The GARDEN BEHIND *the* MOON

Don't get left behind!

STARSCAPE

Let the journey begin . . .

From the Two Rivers
   The Eye of the World: Part One
   by Robert Jordan

Ender's Game
   by Orson Scott Card

Briar Rose
   by Jane Yolen

Mairelon the Magician
   by Patricia C. Wrede

Ender's Shadow
   by Orson Scott Card

To the Blight
   The Eye of the World: Part Two
   by Robert Jordan

The Cockatrice Boys
   by Joan Aiken

Dogland
   by Will Shetterly

The Whispering Mountain
   by Joan Aiken

Orvis
   by H. M. Hoover

And look for . . .

The Dark Side of Nowhere (7/02)
   by Neal Shusterman

Prince Ombra (8/02)
   by Roderick MacLeish

The Magician's Ward (9/02)
   by Patricia C. Wrede

A College of Magics (10/02)
   by Caroline Stevermer

Deep Secret (11/02)
   by Diana Wynne Jones

Pinocchio (11/02)
   by Carlo Collodi

*Another Heaven, Another
   Earth* (12/02)
   by H. M. Hoover

The GARDEN BEHIND the MOON

HOWARD PYLE

A TOM DOHERTY ASSOCIATES BOOK
NEW YORK

This is a work of fiction. All the characters and events portrayed in this book are either products of the author's imagination or are used fictitiously.

THE GARDEN BEHIND THE MOON

A Starscape Book
Published by Tom Doherty Associates, LLC
175 Fifth Avenue
New York, NY 10010

www.starscapebooks.com

ISBN: 0-765-34242-1

First Starscape Edition: June 2002

Printed in the United States of America

0 9 8 7 6 5 4 3 2 1

To the Little Boy in the Moon Garden
this Book is dedicated
by His Father

CONTENTS

The
GARDEN
BEHIND *the*
MOON

Foreword

*W*HEN *you look out across the water at night, after the sun has set and the moon has risen high enough to become bright, then you see a long, glimmering moon-path reaching away into the distance. There it lies, stretching from the moon to the earth, and from the earth to the moon, as bright as silver and gold, and as straight and smooth as a turnpike road.*

There is nothing in all this world that was not made for some reason and for some use—not even the moon-path—but always you must find for yourself the use of a thing and why it was made.

So it is with the moon-path as with everything else. Thousands and thousands of people have seen that long, level stretch of brightness, and have looked out at it, and have thought it was beautiful, but there are very, very few who have ever really found out what is its use.

It looks like a path, and that is what it really is, for if you only know how to do so, you may walk upon it just as easily as you may walk upon a barn floor. All you need to do is to make a beginning, and there you are. After that it is smooth enough walking, and you may skip and play and romp as you choose. Then you may come and go whenever you have a mind to, and if you will take my word for it, it is the most beautiful and wonderful road that a body can travel betwixt here and the land that so few folk ever go to and come back again.

For the moon-path leads straight to the moon. That was why it was built—that a body might go from the brown earth to the moon, and maybe back again.

But why, you may ask, should anybody want to go to the moon? That I will tell you. The reason is that behind the moon there lies the most wonderful, beautiful, never-to-be-forgotten garden that the mind can think of. In it live little children who play and romp, and laugh and sing, and are as merry and happy as the little white lambs in the green meadow in springtime. There they never have trouble and worry; they never dispute nor quarrel; they never are sorry and never cry.

Aye, aye; — that beautiful garden. One time I myself saw it — though in a dream — dim and indistinct, as one might see such a beautiful place through a piece of crooked glass. In it was the little boy whom I loved the best of all. He did not see me, but I saw him, and I think I was looking into the garden out of one of the moon-windows. I was glad to see him, for he had gone out along the moon-path, and he had not come back again.

Perhaps you do not understand what I mean, but maybe you will after you have read this story. For it is all about a little girl who went to the garden behind the moon and lived amid all the beautiful things. Also it is about a little boy who paid a visit to the moon-house, where the Man-in-the-moon lives, and how he too went out the back door into the moon-garden.

It was the Moon-Angel who told the story to me, and now I shall tell it to you just as nearly as I can remember it.

I

The Princess Aurelia

ONCE upon a time—for this is the way that every true fairy story begins—once upon a time there was a King and a Queen who loved one another dearly, and had all that they wanted in the world but one thing. That one thing was a child of their own.

For the house was quiet and silent. There was no sound of silver voice and merry laughter; there was no running hither and thither of little feet; there was no bustle and noise and teasing to make life sweet to live.

For so it is always dull and silent in a house where there are no children.

One day, when the sun was shining as yellow as gold, and the apple-trees were all in bloom—pink and white,—the Queen was walking up and down the garden path, thinking and thinking of how sad it was in the house without any children to make things glad. The tears were in her eyes, and she wiped them away with her handkerchief. Suddenly she heard some one speaking quite near to her: "Lady, lady, why are you so sad?"

The voice came from the apple-tree, and when she looked up among the branches there she saw a beautiful figure dressed all in shining white and sitting amid the apple blossoms, and around the face of the figure it was bright like sunlight.

It was the Moon-Angel, though the Queen did not know that—the Moon-Angel, whom so many people know by a different name and are so afraid of, they know not why. The Queen stood looking up at him, and she felt very still and quiet.

"Why are you so sad, lady?" said the Moon-Angel again.

"Because," said she, "there is no child in the house."

"And if you had a child," said the Moon-Angel, "would that make you happy?"

"Yes," said the Queen.

The Moon-Angel smiled till his face shone bright like

white light. "Then be happy," said he, "For I have come to tell you that you shall have a daughter."

Then, even as the Queen looked, he was gone, and nothing was there but the blossoms and the bright blue sky shining through them.

So by and by a little Princess was born to the King and Queen. And she was a real Princess too, for she came into the world with a golden coronet on her head and a golden star on her shoulder, and so the Queen named her Princess Aurelia.

That same day the Queen died—for the Moon-Angel never brings something into the house but he takes something away with him again. So after all they were more sad and sorrowful than if the Princess had never been born.

Princess Aurelia grew and grew and grew, and the older she grew the more beautiful she grew. But the poor King, her father, was more and more sad every day. For nobody had ever seen such a little child as the Princess. She never cried, but then she never laughed; she never was cross, but then she never smiled; she never teased, but then she never spoke a word; she was a trouble to no one, but then she neither romped nor played. All day she sat looking around her with her beautiful blue eyes, and all night long she slept like an angel, but she might just as well have been a lovely doll as a little child of flesh and blood.

Everybody said that she had no wits, but you shall know better than that when you have read this story and have heard about the moon-garden.

II

The Moon-Calf

*T*HERE was a little boy named David who never had any other name that I know of, unless it was "Silly" David. For he was a moon-calf, and all the other children laughed at him.

A moon-calf? What is a moon-calf?

Ah, little child, little child! That is something you can only learn in one way. For though a world-wise scientist with two pair of short-sighted spectacles on his nose may write a great book upon the differentiation of Human Reason, or another with far-sighted glasses may write a learned disquisition concerning how many microbes there are in a cubical inch of butter-milk, they know no more about what a moon-calf is than my grandmother's bed-post. "Moon-calf!" says such an one; "I do not know what a moon-calf is. There is no such thing. It's nonsense."

If you want to know what a moon-calf really is you will either have to ask the Moon-Angel or else read for yourself in one of his never-to-be-altogether-understood books, where such things are told about, if you only have the wits to understand what is written there.

David was a moon-calf. He carried more wits about him than the little Princess Aurelia, but nevertheless everybody called him a moon-calf. None of the other children would play with him because he was so silly, and so he had always to help his mother about the house, and to look after the baby when she was busy. He lived in a village that stood on the rocky shores of a great sea that stretched far, far away toward the east, so that whenever the moon was round and full, there was the bright moon-path reaching away from the dark earth to the shining disk in the east.

It was a queer, quaint little village in which little David lived. Nearly every one in it, except the minister, the mayor, the schoolmaster and Hans Krout, the crazy cobbler, were fisher folk. It had steep roofs, one climbing up over the other as though to peep over one another's shoulders at the water below. Nearly at the top of the cliff was a church with a white steeple, and beyond that was an open common, where there was grass, and where the geese and the cows fed, and where the boys and the girls played of an evening. Up above on the top of the cliffs was the highway, which ran away across the country and through the fields, past the villages, to the King's city.

David loved the sea as a little lamb loves its mother, and oftentimes when the day was pleasant he would carry the baby down to the shore and sit there on the rocks in the sun and look out across the water. There he would sit hour after hour, and sing to himself and the baby, and think his own thoughts all to himself.

None of the other children were at all like him. They had brown freckled faces and shock heads and strong hands that were nearly always dirty. When they played with one another they would laugh and shout and romp like young colts, and tussle and roll over and over upon the grass. Poor little David would sometimes stand looking at them wonderingly. He would have liked to play with them, but he could not, because he was only a moon-calf, and so simple. Sometimes the little boys, and even the little girls, would laugh at him because he was so foolish, and had a pale face and pale blue eyes, and nursed the baby. Sometimes they called him "simpleton," and sometimes they called him "nurse-a-baby." When they teased him, he would carry the baby off to the rocks and would sit there and look out across the water and think of it all, and maybe want to cry so badly that his throat ached.

III

The Man Who Knew
Less Than Nothing

*B*UT there was one in the village who neither laughed at David nor called him moon-calf. That was Hans Krout, the cobbler. For Hans Krout also was moon-struck. Some of the people of the village used to say that he knew less than nothing, and I dare say what they said was true enough—only sometimes it takes more wits to know less than nothing than to know more than a little.

But Hans Krout had not always been thus. One time he was as world-wise as anybody else. One time he had a wife living with him. He had worked hard when he was young to earn enough money for two people to live upon, and when he had earned it he had married the girl he liked best. They lived together for a while, and then she died. After that Hans Krout became just as he was now, so that some people said he was crazy, and some that he knew less than nothing.

Yet, in spite of what folks said, Hans Krout did know something. He knew more about the moon-path, and the Moon-Angel, and the moon itself than almost anybody.

Little David was very fond of Hans Krout, and when he was not helping his mother, or nursing the baby, or sitting by himself down among the rocks, he used to be in the cobbler's shop watching Hans Krout cobble shoes.

This is how Hans Krout would do it:

He always sat on a bench that had a leather seat to it, and a box at one side. The box was full of brads, and wax-ends, and cobbler's wax, and shoe-pegs, and this and that and what not and the other. Hans Krout would take up a shoe and put into it a wooden foot that he called a last. Then he would fit a piece of sole-leather to the upper and tack it down to the sole of the wooden last. Then he would hold the shoe and all tight between his knees with a strap that went down under his foot. Then he would take his crooked awl and drive it in through the leather sole and out the upper. Then he would stick the two bristles of the wax-end into the hole he had made. Then stretching his arms and drawing the thread about his little fingers, that were always black with shoemaker's wax, he would give a grunt and draw the thread tight.

That is the way he would sew the shoes;—this is the way he would drive the pegs:

He would make a hole with his awl in the sole of the shoe. Then he would stick a little wooden peg into it. Then, rap-tap-tap, he would drive in the peg with his queer, round-faced hammer, and there the peg would be as tight as wax. Then, by and by, he would take his knife and trim off the tops of all the wooden pegs he had driven into the shoe, and rub down the sole till it shone like glass.

Yes, indeed! It is a very wonderful thing to see.

When I was a little boy like David there used to be a cobbler at the old toll-gate under the weeping-willow trees. He had a little black dog, blind of both eyes, whom the Moon-Angel used to lead around hither and thither with a string that nobody could see. I used to go down to the toll-gate and sit there and watch the cobbler cobble shoes just as David used to sit and watch Hans Krout at his work, and to this day I believe it takes more wits to cobble a pair of shoes than to write a big book, and more cleverness to make a good wax-end than to draw a picture with a lead-pencil.

But it was not altogether the shoe cobbling that brought David to the cobbler shop. Hans Krout had a fiddle, and he could play you a tune so sweet and thin and clear that it would make your throat fill up with happiness to listen to him. When he was not busy he used to play the fiddle to David, and David would sit and listen and listen, and the baby would suck its thumb and go to sleep.

But it was not altogether the fiddle either that brought

David to the cobbler shop. For the most wonderful thing about Hans Krout was that he was as full of stories as an egg is full of meat. He could tell you about princes and princesses, and kings and nobles, and lords and giants and hobgoblins, by the hour and by the day, when he was not busy cobbling shoes.

But even this was not the best, for Hans Krout knew ever so much more than these things. He knew all about the Moon-Angel and the moon-path and the moon-garden and the moon-house, and he would sometimes tell the little boy about them. That was the most wonderful of all, for all the other things were only fairy tales, but what he told about moonshine was real.

"Were you ever out along the moon-path yourself?" said David.

"Yes," said Hans Krout. "As true as I sit here. I didn't know how to travel the moon-path at first, for I hadn't learned the trick. All the same I knew that Katherine"— Katherine was Hans Krout's wife—"that Katherine had gone out that way—I mean along the moon-path—with the Moon-Angel. And so I tried and tried, and by and by I learned how to do it. I was down on the shore one night," said Hans Krout, "and there was the moon-path stretching away toward the moon. I knew that this was just the time to take a walk upon it, for the moon was neither too high toward heaven, nor too low toward the earth. There was a wave coming in toward the shore. Right on top of the wave was a crooked bar of moonlight. I knew that was what I had to stand upon, and so I stepped out. But just as I did so I got frightened, and—souse! there I was in the water over head and ears. Well, what of that? I got out and walked home. But I wasn't going to give it up—not I. I went out again another day. There was the moon-path, and there was the wave, and there was the bar of moonlight right atop of the wave. I stepped out again, and this time I wasn't afraid. This time, would you believe it, I didn't fall into the water at all. All the same I had to jump off that wave on to another, for the moonlight was sliding away under my feet. It was as slippery as glass. I jumped to the next wave and to the next and to the next, and then I was all right, and it was like gravel under my feet, and I ran just like you run along the shore where the gravel is. Then by and by the path was like a field of pure light with blades of silver grass, and I ran along just as you do when you run across the fields up on the hills."

"Did you get to the moon?" said David.

"No," said Hans Krout, "not that time. I did get to the moon afterwards, but not that time."

"And what was it like inside of the moon?" asked David.

Hans Krout looked at him and smiled just like a little child when it first awakens—a foolish, silly, simple smile that had no more wits in it than moonshine itself. But it seemed to David that his face grew white and shone bright. He got up, took his fiddle down from the wall, and began to play. He played and played, and little David sat and listened and listened, and the baby slept on and smiled and smiled, until Hans Krout grew tired of playing. Then he laid his fiddle aside and began cobbling shoes, rap-tap-tap!

and the baby came awake and began reaching for David's face. "I wish you'd show me how to walk on the moon-path some time," said David.

"So I will," said Hans Krout, "if you'll be a good boy and mind the baby." Rap-tap-tap! and he drove another peg. Then David heard his mother calling, and he knew he had to go home.

"Moon-calf!" called Tom Stout, as he went along the street. "Moon-calf! Moon-calf! Moon-calf!" called all the other boys and some of the little girls.

Little David looked over his shoulder and laughed. He did not mind how much they called him moon-calf now, for Hans Krout had promised to show him the way to the moon-path, and if he was to play on the moon-path, why, of course he must be a moon-calf.

IV

David in the Water

THERE is only one evening or two at most out of all the twenty-eight and a quarter days that it takes for the moon to change from full to full in which you can travel upon the moon-path. Maybe after a while, and when you get very well acquainted with the way and know just how to set about it, you can travel the moon-path almost whenever you choose. But when you are learning there is, as I said, only one or, at most, two evenings in all the twenty-eight and a quarter days in which you are able to walk out upon it. Those evenings are the second or third after the full of the moon.

I will tell you why this is so. It is because, when the moon is quite full, there is too much daylight to see the moon-path when the moon first rises. And when the moon is too far past the full, there is too much night to see what you are about. For when you are learning to walk upon the moon-path it must be neither daylight nor dark, but just betwixt and between.

So it is that the proper time comes only twice or thrice in all the twenty-eight and a quarter days that it takes the moon to change from full to full.

"Do you know," said Hans Krout to David, "that yesterday was the full of the moon?"

"No, I didn't," said David. "But what of that?"

"Well, I will tell you," said Hans Krout; "this evening will be the best time for me to show you the way to walk out upon the moon-path.

"And will you show me the way tonight?" cried the little boy.

"I will," said Hans Krout, "if you will come to me just after sundown."

Silly little David could hardly believe his ears.

It was not until after sundown that he was able to leave the baby, for the little one cried and fretted, and fretted and cried, until David thought she would never be quiet. But at last she grew still, and fell fast asleep, with her thumb in her mouth. Then he was able to leave her. He came out into the wide air full of the brightness of the twilight that had not yet turned into dusk. There was Hans Krout waiting for him in front of the cobbler shop, shading his eyes with his hand.

"Hi! David," he said, "I have been waiting for you a long, long time."

"Well," said David, "here I am."

"Aye;" said Hans Krout, "there you are. Part of you here, part of you there. That's the way to travel the moon-path."

"I don't know what you mean," said David.

"Don't you?" said Hans Krout, as he looked silly and laughed.

He took David by the hand and led him away up the village street. The little boys and some of the little girls were chasing around and around the grassy common. The geese were cackling, and the cows were lowing, as they were turned out to grass again for the night. Everything looked strange and gray and still in the bright, shadowless twilight. The little boys and the little girls stopped their play and stood looking after Hans Krout and silly little David. Then they began halloing after them. Some of them said:

> *"Hans Krout, Hans Krout,*
> *Your wits are out, your wits are out!"*

And some called, "Moon-calf! Moon-calf!" after David.

David looked up into Hans Krout's face, and he looked so strange, that the little boy was almost frightened.

Thus they walked on together, hand in hand. By and by they left the village behind, and were going along the rocky shore of the sea. They went along, climbing up and down the stony path, until at last they came to a place where David had never been before. Here there was a level shelf of rock, and against the foot of the shelf the waves came in from the sea beyond, rising and falling as though the water was breathing. The light was growing more and more gray. David looked up. There was just one bright star shining in the pallid sky.

Hans Krout stood quite still, holding him by the hand, and looking out toward the purple gray of the east. Little silly David looked up now at the star, and now at Hans Krout's face, and every now and then out across the water. The sky grew darker and darker, and by and by the gray began to change to a dim blue. At first there had been a ruddy light all over the east, as though the sunshine lingered over yonder, after it had left everywhere else. Then, after awhile, that too had faded out, and had changed to blue-gray, and looked almost like a bank of clouds. Then the yellow moon came slowly up, out of nowhere. First the rim of it showed, then the half of it, then the whole of it. Then it floated up, slowly, slowly, into the soft, dark sky, like a golden bubble. Hans Krout's face shone as though the moonlight were shining upon it. "Wait a little," said he.

The moon rose higher and higher, and little David held his breath. There was the moon-path stretching across the water. "Yonder it is," said Hans Krout, "and now is your time."

"What shall I do?" said the little boy.

"Step out like a soldier," said Hans Krout.

"But what shall I step upon?" said David.

"There," said Hans Krout, "don't you see that bar of light on the tip-top of that wave? Step on the top of that, and then you will know what to do next."

Poor little David's head seemed to spin. The wave came closer and closer. "Now, then," said Hans Krout, "step out like a soldier—quick!"

Then David did as Hans Krout told him. He stepped out on the crest of the wave as it came up against the shelf of rock. It seemed to him he stood so for a moment upon the slippery bar of light; then he felt suddenly very much afraid. "Oh, I am falling!" he piped shrilly. Then—souse!— he was struggling and choking in the deep water that gurgled above his head. Once he came up to the top of the water. He saw a glimpse of the moon, and of Hans Krout, and then he was down again—struggling and choking. Somebody caught him by the collar—it was Hans Krout. The next moment he was dragged up on the rock like a drowning kitten. He gasped and choked and gasped again. Then he began to cry. Hans Krout seemed to be frightened at what he had done. He stood for a moment looking at David as he shivered, and shook, and cried; then he turned and walked away back toward the village, with the poor little boy trotting behind him still crying and shivering, the salt water and the salt tears trickling down his poor little thin face.

Hans Krout did not stop at David's house to tell them how it happened. He hurried home almost as though he were running away. David's father was sitting mending his nets. He looked up as David came creeping in, wet and shivering. "Thunder and lightning!" said David's father, taking the pipe out of his mouth, "what has happened to you, little child?"

"I tried to walk on the moon-path," said little David, "and I fell through it into the water. That is all."

"Tried to walk on the moon-path!" said David's father. "What does the child mean?"

"Hans Krout took me out," said David, "and showed me the moon-path, and how to walk on it; but when I stepped on it I got frightened and slipped through into the water."

David's father sat staring at him, holding his pipe in his crooked brown fingers. "What is all this nonsense?" said he. "Hans Krout, is it?—showing you the moon-path? Well, you shall go with Hans Krout no more, for he is crazy and knows not what he does. Here, Margaret, take the child and put him to bed. Why, he is cold to the marrow! Moon-path! The crazy shoemaker will be the death of somebody yet!"

So David's mother put him to bed, and David cried himself to sleep.

V

The Moon-Angel

*H*ANS Krout seemed almost afraid of David for a while after that. He would not speak to the little boy on the street, and even when David came to the cobbler-shop he would not play his fiddle. Neither would he tell David the story of the Princess in the Glass Hill with three lions at the door, and the Prince with the red band around his wrist. Once he had promised to tell the story, but now he would not. He just stitched and rapped and cobbled at his shoes as though he had wits for nothing else.

"Are you angry with me, Hans?" said David.

"I am not," said Hans.

"What is it, then?" said David.

"It is nothing," said Hans.

"But will you not tell me the story?" said David.

"I will not," said Hans.

"Why not?" said David.

"Because the Master Cobbler has stopped up my wits with shoemaker's wax," said Hans.

"Who is the Master Cobbler?" said David.

"No matter," said Hans.

David sat for a long time looking at Hans. "Will you show me the moon-path again some time?" said he, after a while.

"I do not know," said Hans Krout, without looking up, "that depends."

"Depends upon what?" said David.

"Depends upon the Master Cobbler," said Hans.

So all that month Hans Krout was dull and silent and stupid, and would hardly speak to David. He would not even look at the baby, and so David had to go off by himself to find amusement elsewhere.

There was a place down by the sea-shore where he always went at such times; he called it his sea-house. There was a little sandy, gravelly floor, with the rocks all around it. There was a pool of water full of sea-weed, and strange things that were alive—sea-anemones and crabs and shellfish. Everything smelt salt, and out beyond you could see the sea, with the sun shining and sparkling and dancing on the waves. That was where David used to go by himself with the baby to be alone.

It was there that he first saw the Moon-Angel.

This is how it was: the baby had been fretting and crying, and David's mother was very cross, for she had been sitting up the night before with poor little Barbara Stout, who was very sick, so that Barbara's mother might get a little wink of sleep. So David took the baby to make her quiet, and as soon as he had done so, she stuck her thumb in her mouth and stopped crying. The sun was shining warm and bright, and David took the baby down to his sea-house. The wind was blowing, and he sat looking out across the sea and at the big waves that rose and fell as though the water were breathing long and deep,—the big waves that soughed and sighed among the rocks as though the sea were murmuring in its sleep. All over the bosom of the waves there were little wavelets that leaped and skipped and winked and twinkled as the breeze came chasing them. The sea-gulls hovered and skimmed overhead, looking down at David and laughing "ha-ha-ha" in the sunlight.

So there David sat and looked out across the wide, bright, deep, breathing water and the dancing little waves, and the baby lay with her thumb in her mouth, staring up into the blue sky.

Then he saw the Moon-Angel for the first time.

"Why not try the moon-path to-night?" said a voice behind David. David turned his head quickly, and the baby turned her head also, for she heard the voice as well as David.

David thought at first it was Hans Krout, the cobbler, but it was not. It was the Moon-Angel.

David knew who it was as soon as he set eyes on him, for David was of that kind who can see more through the square hole of a millstone than t'other side of it, and so he knew it was the Moon-Angel as soon as he set eyes on him. The Moon-Angel's face shone as white as silver, and his hair floated out like a bright cloud around the moon. He had on a long, dim, silver-white robe that reached to his bare feet, and though the robe was perfectly plain and dim silver-white, yet it sparkled all over with little stars, just as the dim silver-white gray sky sparkles here and there with stars when the moon is full.

That is what David saw.

To most people the Moon-Angel appears terrible. For there are few folk, unless it is a moon-calf like David, who can see him in his true shape, with his face shining brightly, and his hair flowing, and his dim silver-white robe sparkling with stars.

David took off his hat, and the baby laughed without taking her finger out of her mouth. "I would like to try again," said he; "I did try once, but I couldn't do it."

"Why?" said the Moon-Angel, and he smiled till his face shone white like the moon.

"I got frightened and fell into the water," said David.

"But you shouldn't have been frightened," said the Moon-Angel.

"But I couldn't help it," said David.

"And what did Hans Krout do then?" asked the Moon-Angel.

"He went home," said David, "and he's never said a

word about the moon-path from that day to this."

Again the Moon-Angel smiled, and his face shone brighter than ever. "Well," said he, "Hans Krout is a very good man and a great friend of mine. He can show you the way, and there is no man about here who can show you the way. Go to him and tell him that he is to show you the way to walk on the moon-path tonight."

"Who shall I tell him sent me?" said David.

"Tell him the Master Cobbler sent you," said the Moon-Angel.

"Oh, yes," said David, "now I know whom he meant by the Master Cobbler."

"Yes," said the Moon-Angel, "that is right. Well, then, maybe I will see you after a while. Just now I am very busy. Good-by."

David still looked at the Moon-Angel. The Moon-Angel glimmered and glimmered and faded and was gone, and where he had been was nothing but the sky and the rocks. David almost wondered whether he had seen the Angel or not—whether what he had seen was really the Angel's face or just the bright sky shining between the rocks.

Afterwards he knew well enough he had really seen the Moon-Angel, for it was just after this that little Barbara Stout's mother began crying and clapping her hands together, and that the neighbors came in and found that the little sick girl had died.

But David knew nothing of that. He got up and, carrying the baby, went off to Hans Krout and told him what he had seen and what the Moon-Angel had said to him. "Yes," said Hans Krout, "that was His Serene Highness, the Master Cobbler, for sure and certain. Well, well, since he says so, I will take you down to the moon-path tonight, and we will try it again."

"And what do you suppose the Moon-Angel was doing about here?" said David.

"He came to take the little sick Barbara away to the moon-garden," said Hans Krout. Then he took down his fiddle and began to play for the first time in a month, and David sat and listened, and the baby went to sleep.

That night Hans Krout led David down to the moon-path again, for it was the day after the full moon. They went off together just as they had done before; out of the village and along the stony path among the boulders, until they came to the same place where they had been before—the flat rock against which the waves came in from the wide sea beyond. Again they sat there waiting and waiting while the sky grew from rosy to gray, and from gray to purple, and from purple to dusk; until the moon rose as yellow as honey over the edge of the ocean; until it floated like a bubble up into the sky—then there was the moon-path just as it had been before.

"Now, then," said Hans Krout, "there comes a good bar of light on the top of yonder wave. Remember the Moon-Angel—quick!—step out like a soldier. There you are—now, then!"

David did think of the Moon-Angel, and he stepped upon the wave almost without knowing what he was doing. This time *he* was not afraid, and the next moment there he was standing upon the bar of light. It seemed to slip and slide under his feet as though it were alive. He nearly fell, but he did not remember to be afraid. Another wave came with another twisting, wriggling bar of light upon the top of it. David stepped upon it just in time to save himself from falling. Then another wave came, and he stepped upon it; then another and another wave. Each broken piece of light was closer and closer to him than the one he had left, and almost before he knew it he found himself running across what was no longer broken bars of light but what seemed to him to be shifting, changing gravel of shining gold.

He looked up; the moon had not risen any further out of the water. There it hung, almost round and almost full, just above the edge of the horizon—a great bubble of brightness. Now then David was away even from the gravel, and he found himself running across what seemed to be a great field of light covered all over with soft sparkles of silver grass. Everything shimmered, and quivered, and glistened around him, and he felt the light rise up against his eyes and his face. The breeze blew through his hair. He felt so happy, he did not know what to do. He skipped and capered just as a little lamb skips and capers on the grass. It seemed to David as though the moon was coming towards him; it appeared to grow bigger and bigger—he was really getting closer and closer to the moon. It was no longer like a bubble; it was like a great round globe of light. Then, almost before he knew, he was at the edge of the horizon, with nothing beyond him but emptiness. And there was the great moon rising above him as big as a church.

David stood quite still and looked up at it. Click-clack! What was that? Suddenly a half-door opened and there stood a little old man, as gray as the evening, with long white hair and queer clothes, and a face covered all over with cobwebs of silver wrinkles. It was the Man-in-the-moon, and he was smoking a long pipe of tobacco.

"How do you do, David?" said he. "Will you come in?"

"Why, yes," said David, "I would like to."

"That is good," said the Man-in-the-moon, and he opened the other half of the door. "Now! Give me your hand."

The Man-in-the-moon reached down to David, and David reached up to the Man-in-the-moon. "Now, then!—A long step," said the Man-in-the-moon—and there was David in the doorway of the moon-house.

Then the moon rose slowly, slowly, up into the sky and floated away, and the Man-in-the-moon shut the door— click!—clack!

VI

The Moon-House

*U*PON my word, I sometimes think I would rather go to the moon-house than almost anywhere else I know of. I have read all about it in the Moon-Angel's book, and know pretty well just what it is like—that is why I would like so well to see it. Some people are dreadfully afraid of the moon-house; it seems to them—to be white and cold and awful. That is because they only see the outside of it, and do not know what is within. It is not what such people fancy it to be; it is a calm, beautiful, lovely place, from the back-door of which you step into the other side of nowhere. I used to be just as much afraid of the moon-house as the most foolish of them. Sometimes I would dream about it at night, and it seemed to me to be a great white emptiness, from which you could see nothing at all, and in which you could not hear anything, or feel anything, or know anything. Then one day the Moon-Angel came to me with his book under his arm. "Would you like to know about the moon-house?" said he.

"Yes; I would," said I.

"Very well," said he, "then look!"

He opened his book, and I looked over his shoulder and read it. It was all about the moon-house, and I read, and read, and read. Since then I have never been afraid of the moon-house, for now I know pretty well what it is, and that it is a most wonderful, strange, curious, odd, fanciful, beautiful place, that one can get into for the sake of getting out again.

For, of course, no one wants to live in the moon-house forever—that is, no one except the Man-in-the-moon, and he does not mind it any more than a cat minds living in the kitchen.

The Man-in-the-moon led David up the front stairs into the moon, and everything shone as white as bright light. Up the stairs they went, and up the stairs, a long, long way. By and by they came out into a great round room, and it was the first floor of the moon-house. It was the moon-kitchen, and there the Man-in-the-moon does all his cooking and brewing and patching and mending, for it is full of all sorts of odds and ends of things that men have seen and heard about and forgotten—and they are ten thousand times more numerous than the things that men have seen and heard about and remembered.

There the Man-in-the-moon sat down and looked at David, and David stared at the Man-in-the-moon. There was something about him that looked—looked—David did not know whether it was like Hans Krout or the Moon-Angel—and yet he looked like neither. He was just the Man-in-the-moon, and he looked no more like Hans Krout or the Moon-Angel than I do.

Then the Man-in-the-moon began laughing. "Well," said he, "here you are, David."

"Yes," said David, "here I am."

"And how do you like it?" said the Man-in-the-moon.

David looked all around him. "I like it very well," said he—"if only I were sure of somebody to look after the baby down below there."

"Have no fear of that," said the Man-in-the-moon. "You have left a part of yourself down there behind you, and that will look after the baby as well as you ever were able to do yourself."

"What do you mean?" said David. "What part of me have I left down there?"

"You have left your hat and clothes and shoes," said the old man, "and nobody down there knows otherwise than that you are in them."

"And will they look after the baby as well as I would do?" asked David.

"They will," said the Man-in-the-moon.

"Then I shall like it here very well," said David, "at least for a while."

"Would you like to go upstairs and look out of the windows?" said the old man. "That is the first thing that all the folk who come here ask to do."

"And what do they see?" said David.

"They see the inside-of-nothing-at-all," said the Man-in-the-moon.

"I would like to see that," said David.

"Come along, then," said the Man-in-the-moon.

He led the way up another flight of stairs to the second story. There was a great room with a floor as level and as smooth as glass, and there were twelve great windows of crystal that looked out of it. From the windows you could see all that you ever heard tell of and more beside, for from those windows you can, as the Man-in-the-moon said, see the inside-of-nothing-at-all.

"Come here," said the Man-in-the-moon, "and you may look out of this window."

He raised the curtain as he spoke, and David came and looked out.

Now, when you look out of a window of a common house, you see things far away. That is because you are not in the moon-house looking out of a moon-window. When David looked out of the window, he saw things very close at hand. That was because he was in the moon-house looking out of the moon-window, and not in a common house looking out of a common window.

What David Saw

He found himself suddenly upon a wide river, the stream moving slowly and sluggishly between the banks, where the grass and weeds stood straight and as tall as a man's head. Overhead was a cloudless sky, in which the sun shone as hot as a flame of fire. There was a boat coming down the river with a queer crooked sail, spread in hopes of catching a breeze, though there was no wind blowing. Three men were rowing the boat, and the oars dipped and flashed in the sunlight.

It was all very strange to David, and yet it was all singularly familiar to him. He could not think why it should be so familiar until he remembered that he had heard Ned Strong, the sailorman, tell his father about this very place, which he had seen in his travels, and all that had happened there. Then David knew it was a place called Africa.

Dear, dear; how hot the sun shone! David wished he had brought his hat. When you looked out across the tall grass, the level stretch seemed to tremble and quiver in the heat. It was all grass, grass as far as the eye could see.

The boat came nearer and nearer, just as Ned Strong had said. Then it was very close, and David could see everything in it, just as though he were looking over the side of a ship as Ned Strong had done. In the boat, beside those who were rowing, were a great lot of black people—men and women—each without a single stitch of clothes upon his or her body. All the poor black people were fastened together with great, long ropes, and each wore a collar of wood, to which the rope was fastened.

David remembered that Ned Strong had said that these were slaves, and he felt almost more sorry for them than he had felt in all his life before. The poor slaves sat there staring straight before them. They looked scared and starved and thin, and their ribs were like barrel hoops, just as Ned Strong had said, their bodies hollow, and their arms and necks like skin and bones. But there they sat patiently without moving, and the flies crawled over them, and they did not have the spirit to brush them away. There was one young woman who sat with her baby lying upon her knees. She sat the most quietly and patiently of all, for she was dead, though nobody knew it. By and by, a man dressed in a loose robe, and with a fez on his head, came down the long board that ran the length of the boat. When he came to the woman he stopped and looked at her, and saw that she was dead, though the baby was still alive. Then he called to some of his men, who came and loosened the rope about her, for it was of no use to keep the woman any longer, and so they threw her overboard. David was crying.

The baby still lay in the boat, and then the man with the loose robe and the fez picked it up, and threw it also into the water after the mother, for it too was of no use. David screamed aloud.

Then, lo and behold! everything was gone like a flash. What David saw now was the bottom of the river, and all around was nothing but water. There were great beds of long water grass twisting and moving slowly as the slow river water drifted past. Overhead David could see the round bottom of the boat as it moved slowly away, the oars still dipping and making round golden rings on the smooth surface of the river overhead. It was very cool and pleasant down there at the bottom of the river, under the water, and the black woman and the black baby lay not far from one another, each in a bed of soft green water grass.

Then somebody came walking along through the beds of long, cool water grasses. It was the Moon-Angel. He came to where the black woman lay, and he took her by the hand. Then she arose and stood looking about her. The Moon-Angel picked up the baby and laid it in her arms. "Come," said he, "we must be going."

The black mother, with her baby in her arms, followed the Moon-Angel as he led them up out of the water into a garden, where there were children playing. They stopped playing as the Moon-Angel led the black woman with the baby through the garden. David looked about him; it was a very wonderful garden. There were flowers everywhere, and there was a meadow in the distance, and a row of trees along by a river, and far away beyond that, a great city, sparkling white in the sunlight against the still blue sky. Then David understood that the children belonged to the city, and that their teacher had brought them out into the garden to play.

(He did not then know that it was one of the gardens behind the moon.)

The children joined David, and followed along after the

black woman and her baby and the Moon-Angel, and their teachers did not forbid them. The black woman looked around at the children and laughed, and they also laughed.

"Where are you going?" called David to the black woman. "Where is the Moon-Angel going to take you?"

The woman answered him, but even though he was a moon-calf, David could not understand what she said, for she spoke in no words that fitted to any speech except the speech of a very few.

By and by David found that the children were no longer following the Moon-Angel and the woman with her baby. Then he heard somebody calling him. He looked around; it was the Man-in-the-moon. "Stop!" called the Man-in-the-moon. "Come back! You must go no further."

"Why not?" said David.

"Because you've got to the end of nowhere," said the Man-in-the-moon, "and no one can go further than that unless the Moon-Angel takes him."

"But I'd like to see where she goes," said David. Then the Man-in-the-moon ran forward and caught him by the coat and pulled him back. As he did so, there suddenly came a flash of great light that shone all around and dazzled David's eyes. In the blinding light, David could see nothing at all, and he stood there quite still, trembling and frightened. Then he heard something like the sound of thunder in the distance. But it was not that; it was the sound of thousands and thousands of voices, singing in a multitudinous cadence, that was like the rushing of many waters, and like the vast hum of far-away music, and like the distant pealing of thunder. The Moon-Angel and the woman and the baby were gone, and there was nothing but the light and the sound.

Ah! yes, little child. For there is as much joy and gladness over one poor black woman who enters into that place as there is over the whitest empress who ever walked the earth of Christendom.

Suddenly something was closed, and David found himself inside the moon-house. The Man-in-the-moon had drawn the curtain over the window,—that was all.

"But where did the woman and the baby go?" asked David.

"That," said the Man-in-the-moon, "you will have to ask the Moon-Angel himself sometime when you meet him. But tell me, did you like what you saw?"

"It was very beautiful," said David. "But Ned Strong did not tell my father about all that I have seen. He only told about those poor slaves, and how the woman and the little baby were thrown into the water.

The Man-in-the-moon laughed. "Aye, aye," said he, "that was because he saw the outside of things. If Ned Strong could only come here to the moon-house, and look out of the second story window, as you have done, he would not have bothered himself about the outside, which is no more to the inside of things than the shell of the egg is to the meat."

"But," said David, "why did there have to be such an outside? Why did the poor black woman have to be ill-treated, and starve and die, and why did the poor little black baby have to be thrown alive into the water? The other part was beautiful, but that was dreadful and sad."

The Man-in-the-moon laughed again. "Because," said he, "everything that has an inside must have an outside as well, for there can be no inside unless there is an outside. And this is true, little child: the more sad the outside, the more beautiful almost always is the inside. But, come, you must go to work now. You have spent enough time looking out of the window. Tomorrow night you shall see something else, but now it is time to go to work."

Then the Man-in-the-moon led David up to the third story of the moon-house, where there was nothing above him except the hollow, empty sky. The first thing David saw was a great basket full of stars of all sorts and sizes and kinds. Some shone white, and some blue, and some rosy red. The light shone from them so that all about was a mist of brightness.

David stared with all his eyes, as well he might, for there are few indeed who get into the third story of the moon-house and see what David saw—that great basket full of bright stars.

Beside the basket was a bundle of lamb's-wool. "There is your work," said the Man-in-the-moon. "It is to polish the stars with lamb's-wool, so that they may shine brightly when the moon wanes and the sky is dark once more."

David sat down on the wooden bench and took up a big blue star. He blew his breath upon it and rubbed it with the lamb's-wool, and as he rubbed it it grew brighter and brighter, and pulsed and glowed and throbbed with light as though it were alive. David did not know how beautiful a star could be until he held it in his own hand and rubbed it with lamb's-wool.

I dare say that you will hardly believe that this is the truth. I dare say there are some wise folk, each of whom wears two pairs of spectacles upon his nose, who will tell you that it is all nonsense. Well, well, maybe it is all nonsense, but sometimes there is more solid truth in a little nonsense than in a whole peck of potatoes. All that you have to do is to look up into the sky when the moon is full, and there you will see for yourself that there are scarcely any stars to be seen, and those few so dull and dim that they hardly twinkle at all. That is because somebody in the moon is polishing the others with lamb's-wool to make them bright for the time when the sky is dark again.

There are some few stars that even those in the moon do not polish. Those are given to the sun children to burnish in the sun-oven.

This is not all nonsense.

VII

The Moon-Garden

*S*o David lived in the moon-house for twelve days, and every day, when he had no work to do, he looked out of a moon window. And each time he looked out of a window he saw something different from that which he had seen the day before. One time he saw a tropical forest, where the liana vines hung from the trees like great curtains, covered all over with red and yellow and blue flowers, and out beyond the edge of the forest was the sea, where the mangroves grew down by the water's edge, and where black crabs, with little red spots peppered over their bodies, twiddle their legs and crawled in and out among the tall, thin roots. The wind rushed and rattled through the palm leaves, and all sorts of birds and strange insects flitted and hummed and buzzed about him. For it was not at all like looking out of a common window. It seemed to David as though he were walking in the forest itself with all these living things buzzing and humming and moving about him. Ah! it is something worth while to look out of a moon window, I can tell you, little child. You yourself will see how it is some day, for everybody looks out of a moon window sooner or later, and this is not all nonsense either.

At another time David saw the icebergs glittering bright and transparent with sapphire and green and red light as they floated in the dark northern seas. He was, it seemed to him, walking on the ice-floes, and there were herds of seals and walrus scattered like black patches along the white shore. The northern lights waved like white and violet banners in the air, and queer little Eskimo folk—men, women, and children—clad all in furs, crept in and out of their ice houses.

At another time it was as though he was aboard of a great ship, with its sails spread white and round, as it went sailing away toward the Indies; plunging and yawing across the ocean, with clouds of foam and spray under the bow, and with little Mother Carey's chickens flitting from wave to wave astern, waiting for the cook to throw good things overboard. The great waves rose and fell, and the air was full of the sound of rushing waters. The tall masts with their tangled maze of rigging swung back and forth across the sky, and the salt air swept dank and cool across the deck. It was famous sailing weather.

All these things David saw out of the windows of the moon-house—and it was just as though he was living in the midst of them, as you live in the midst of things when you are out of doors. But I have told you only the outside of what he saw. Always David would see the inside as well—how the great tangled, useless tropical forest was working and working with all its might and main to get things in such order that man might live there some day or other; how the great brown earth lay fast asleep under the arctic ice fields, waiting until its time should come to work as the tropical forests were working; how the great ship, that the captain, and the supercargo, and the sailors thought was carrying calico and cotton cloth to the coolies, was really and truly carrying old things to the Moon-Angel, so that he might make them over into new things again. These were the things that David saw.

So the days passed, and every evening the Man-in-the-moon came and took the stars that David had polished and stuck them up in the sky where they belonged. You may see that for yourself if you watch; for as the moon passes the full, the sky grows darker and more dark, and the stars grow greater and greater in number, as the Man-in-the-moon puts them back in their places.

And now David began to see the very strangest part of the strange things that concern the moon-house.

Each day the moon-house grew less and less bright. By and by, half the moon-house was dark and half shone as white as shining silver. By and by three fourths of the moon was dark and only one fourth was bright. By and by the moon-house was all dark except just a little rim of silver light.

And each day there were fewer and fewer of the twelve windows open. By and by there were six of them closed and six of them open. By and by there were nine of them closed and only three of them open. By and by they were all closed, and the second story was darkened as a room is darkened in summer time when you are sent to take a nap in the afternoon.

And each day there were fewer and fewer stars in the basket in the third story. By and by the basket was half emptied. By and by it was three quarters emptied. By and by it was all emptied but just a few scattered stars in the bottom. At last they were all gone, and the Man-in-the-moon came up-stairs and shut the trap-door that led up from below into the third story, and locked it with a padlock, and put the key in his pocket.

He did this because nobody is allowed to be in the third story of the moon unless they have stars to polish. That is the way it is in the moon,—and that is the way it is everywhere else and with everybody.

So, now, the moon was all closed and darkened, and everything was a dim twilight, just as it is in a house that is closed and darkened in the day time. It was of no use to go up into the second story now, for the windows were all closed. So David spent all of his time down in the moon-kitchen, watching the Man-in-the-moon as he stitched and patched and cobbled and tinkered and mended at all the queer odds and ends of things that people have seen or heard of and forgotten about. When the Man-in-the-moon was not doing that, he was cooking or frying at the stove or making up the beds; and when he was not doing that, he was reading the almanac by candle-light. As for stories—clever as was Hans Krout at telling stories, the Man-in-the-moon knew ten times more than he, and could play the fiddle beside, so that, after all, that time of moon darkness was anything but a dull time for David.

Then one day a wonderful thing happened. Somebody was singing in the second story of the moon-house, and when David looked up the stair toward the door-way above, he saw a light shining through the cracks and the keyhole as though very bright candles were burning on the other side.

David sat and looked, and listened and wondered. "What is that?" said he to the Man-in-the-moon.

"Go and see for yourself," said the Man-in-the-moon, without looking up from the almanac.

"By myself?" said David.

"Of course," said the Man-in-the-moon. "How else would you go?"

Then David got slowly up from the cricket where he sat and went up the tall, steep stairs that led to the second story of the moon-house. He did not know what was about to happen next. He stopped and listened at the door. The singing was louder and louder; it sounded like a whole hive full of golden bees humming in tune. The light through the cracks and the key-hole shone brighter and brighter; it was like the light of seven hundred and ten wax candles shining in a dark room. David opened the door a little crack and peeped in.

The room was all full of brightness, and there was the Moon-Angel, himself.

He was standing at an open window that David had never seen before, and he stood gazing out of it into the dark, still, fathomless sky. He was gazing, gazing at one bright star that shone, now red, now blue, and flickered and blazed, and then shone red and then blue again. There he stood gazing, gazing at the star, and in his eyes were two shining stars just like the one at which he was looking, and the two stars in his eyes shone now red, now blue, and flickered and blazed, and then shone red, and then blue again. And all the time that the Moon-Angel gazed at the star he sang to himself a soft, low song, such as you will never hear until the clay stoppers are taken out of your ears. That was the music that David heard humming like a hive of golden bees. The Moon-Angel never turned his face or looked anywhere but up at the bright star, but as David gazed at him he knew that the Moon-Angel was looking at him, even though he was looking so steadily at that bright star of changing red and blue. And though the Moon-Angel never stopped gazing, he spoke to David as though there were no one else in the world. "How do you do, David?" said he. "Come in and shut the door."

"Thank you, sir," said David. He came in and shut the door behind him. "What are you doing?" said he.

"I am making old things new," said the Moon-Angel.

David stood and looked at the Moon-Angel, and the Moon-Angel stood and gazed at the star and sang to himself. That is one way he makes old things new. He did not move so much as a hair, and yet it was as he said. All the time he was making old things over into new things.

That is what the Moon-Angel does, and that is why he was made, and set a-going—so that he might save a body from growing old forever.

"Well, David," said he at last, "you have been a good boy and have done your work well. Now you shall have three days' holiday."

"Thank you, sir," said David. "And where shall I go for my holiday?"

"You shall," said the Moon-Angel, "go into the moon-garden. That is the best place out of the world in which to play."

"The moon-garden?" said David. "That sounds well, but how shall I get there?"

"Down the back stairs and out the back door," said the Moon-Angel.

"Thank you, sir," said David. "When shall I go?"

"You may go now," said the Moon-Angel.

"Thank you, sir," said David again. "But where are the back stairs?"

"Look for yourself and see," said the Moon-Angel.

David looked about him, and there they were—the back stairs. He wondered that he had not seen them before, just as we all do when we suddenly stumble upon them—those back stairs of the moon.

There they were, and the strangest part of it was that, now David had found them, there was no other way out of the second story of the moon-house.

Yes, it was very strange; but it is as true as the sun in the blue sky. And as it was with David, so it is with every one: as soon as you find the back stairs of the moon-house, you lose sight of the front stairs, and there is no other way out of the second story; and when you find the front stairs, you may hunt until your head spins, but not so much as a single step of the back stairs can you find. You can only see one flight of stairs at a time;—either it is the front stairs, or else it is the back stairs. You can find whichever you choose, but you cannot find them both at the same time. If you choose to find the front stairs, there they are, and there is the moon-path and the brown world far away, and you can get back there whenever you choose, if the tide is right. But if you look for the back stairs, there they are, and the front stairs are gone, and whither the back stairs lead, you must find for yourself.

All this, I say, is as true as the sun in the blue sky. Yes, it is; and you must not believe poets when they tell you it is not true. The fact is, that many, many people, who do not know what they are talking about, vow and declare that there are no back stairs to the moon, and when you tell them there are back stairs, they laugh and sneer, and giggle and snicker and flout at you, and, maybe, call you a moon-calf, just as the little boys and the little girls in the village called David a moon-calf. That is because such folk do not choose to look for the back stairs, and so they never find them.

But now, there they were, and David knew that they must lead somewhere, for the stairs were made for the people to go up and down. So downstairs he went—down, down, down. The stairs were narrow, and he had to feel his way in the milk-whiteness, but he went on, down, down, and by and by he saw a bright light shining from the other side through the cracks of the door, just as the light had shone from the second story, when he had been in the moon-kitchen, and the Moon-Angel up above. And now that he had come to the door, he heard the sound of voices on the other side, and they were the voices of children, laughing and playing. David stopped and listened for a little while, and thought to himself: "There are little children there, and they are playing with one another. They will not want me to play with them, for all the children call me moon-calf, and if I go there, maybe they will just laugh and flout at me, as they used to do down in the village." So he thought at first he would go back again up into the moon, but then he said to himself: "No, the Moon-Angel would not have told me to come unless he wanted me to do so."

He put up his hand and felt for the lock. He found it and pressed the latch. Click-clack! the door opened a crack. Then he pushed it open wider. Then he stepped out into the brightness beyond.

If you want to know how he felt at first, just stay in a dark room for a half hour, and then step out into the bright sunlight. David saw nothing at all but the dazzling light, that was neither like the light of the sun nor like the light of a cloudy day. He smelt flowers and heard children's voices, but he could see nothing. He put up his hand to his eyes to shelter them, and stood winking and blinking and shrinking. For a moment the children's voices still rose in a great loud babble, then suddenly they ceased, and everything was hushed and still. David knew that they were all looking at him. "Now they will call me moon-calf," he thought to himself.

But they did not. "Oh-h-h!" said the voices, and they rose higher and higher, and shriller and shriller. "Oh-h-h-here is a new little boy!" and then David could look around him.

Yes; there he was in the midst of the moon-garden, but there was no moon-house in sight. There was a broad level lawn of grass with a sun-dial and rose bushes. Beyond the lawn there were trees rich both with flowers and fruit. Over the tops of the trees he could see a long, bright-red brick house, with a row of windows that shone in the sun, and a sloping roof, and a tower with a clock, and a brass weather-vane, that burned like a spark of yellow fire against the blue sky above. It was very beautiful, but David only just looked at it. That was all; for there all around him was a circle of children standing looking at him with big round eyes. There was none of them older than twelve years, and none of them younger than three, because a child of less than three years is too young to come into this part of the moon-garden, and a child past twelve is too old to be there.

So nobody but children between three and twelve years old are allowed here, except the teachers. So these children—there were twenty-five or thirty of them—stood looking at David with great round eyes, and with them was the most beautiful lady that David had ever seen—a lady with a soft, gentle face, and smooth hair, and eyes as blue as the sky. She was the teacher. She too was looking at him with gentle blue eyes, then she reached out and laid her hand very gently upon him and looked into his face. "Where did you come from, little boy?" said she.

"I came out of the moon," said David.

"To be sure you did," said she. "And now I see that you have been polishing the stars, have you not?"

"Yes," said David. "With lamb's-wool, ma'am," he added.

"I knew you had," said the lady, "for I saw them shining in your eyes. And you have come here for a holiday, have you not?"

"Yes ma'am," said David; "the Moon-Angel sent me."

"To be sure he did," said the beautiful lady. "Very well, then; run along and play with the other children, for supper will be ready by and by."

"But won't they call me moon-calf?" said David.

The beautiful lady laughed; the sweetest, gentlest laugh. "No, indeed," said she; "they will never call you moon-calf, for all the children here are moon-calves. But now run away and play, children."

Then all the other children scampered away, shouting and laughing, and David ran after them, not feeling even yet quite sure that they wanted him. Beside that, he did not know how to play as other children played.

The biggest boy of the lot was just about David's age. "You shall be our king," said he, "because the Moon-Angel sent you here and because you have polished the stars. There isn't one among us who has done that."

"I looked out of the moon-window, too," said David.

"Oh-h-h-h!" cried all the little children, and they came crowding up around him, and some of the littlest of them pushed up against him. "What did you see?"

Then David told them some of the things he had seen out of the second-story windows, and they all listened in silence.

David thought he had never been so happy in all his life before, for all the children called him their king and asked him what he chose to play; and they listened to him, and did as he told them, and nobody called him a moon-calf.

So they romped and played and shouted until supper time. Then a bell rang, and there was a supper of bread and butter and honey in bright blue china plates, and milk in blue china cups. The supper was spread on a long table under the shade of the trees. The birds sang in the branches over their heads, and bees buzzed and hummed in the flowers, and the sloping afternoon sun shone warm through the leaves and blossoms, and the clock bell in the tower struck five, and everything was as sweet and happy and tranquil as an evening in May time. David's heart swelled so full of happiness that it almost ached.

After supper was over the beautiful lady sat on the grass

and read them wonderful stories out of a picture book, and the children crowded around her and peeped over her shoulder and across her arms, and got into her lap and scrambled over her, and she never once scolded them,— even when they trod on her beautiful dress. The picture book was full of the most wonderful fairy tales that ever you heard in your life, and the pictures were painted in colors as real as life. And the most wonderful part of the book was that the pictures moved just as real things move. The leaves and branches of the trees moved as though the wind were blowing, the flags on the castle fluttered and waved, the giants walked about, the lions wagged their tails, and you could almost hear them roar, the boats sailed across the water, and the beautiful Princess leaned out and waved her handkerchief, and the Prince galloped up in a cloud of dust.

David had never seen such a wonderful book in all his life before, and he fairly held his breath as he looked at the pictures and listened to the wonderful stories the beautiful lady read aloud to the children.

Then came the twilight, soft and gray, and time for the children to go to bed. The bedroom was in the red brick house—a great, long room, with two rows of small white beds, that smelt of old lavender and dry rose leaves, and all sorts of sweet things. There the children were put to bed, and nobody scolded them, though they laughed and talked and romped to their heart's content, and jumped up and down on the beds, and climbed in and out of them. Every now and then, when their romping and shouts grew louder and louder, the beautiful lady would say, "Hush, hush!" in her gentle voice, but that was all. So they played until they were tired, and then went to sleep—all but David.

He lay quite still, feeling happy—so happy and quiet. He watched the beautiful lady as she moved silently through the room, putting the children's clothes to rights, and when she saw that David was looking at her, with his big blue eyes, she came and stooped over him and kissed him.

Then the great moon rose full and round and yellow, and looked in at the tall windows, and shone in David's face—for when there is no moon at all on the brown earth, then it is full moon in the moon-garden.

VIII

Phyllis

*T*HERE was one little child that David liked better than all the other children; her name was Phyllis, and she was a princess—for she wore a golden coronet. Here eyes were as blue as the sky, and her hair was as yellow as gold, and her lips were as red as corals, and her teeth were as white as pearls, and her laugh was like the tinkle of water, and she had the sweetest, shyest, prettiest little ways that ever any little maiden had. David used to stand and look at her, and look at her. It was almost as though he were afraid of her, but it really was not that. Phyllis knew very well when David was looking at her, for she would look slyly back at him out of the corner of her eyes, and then, maybe, she would burst out laughing like a peal of silver bells, and perhaps run away. She used to sit beside David at table, and he would always choose her out of the ring when they were playing "There were three Knights a-riding." And when they would sing—for they used to sing together every morning—he always stood beside her, and it seemed to him that their voices matched so perfectly together, that it made his ears ring as though a glass bell had been struck. Then she would look at him, and he would look at her; and the beautiful lady would look at them both, and if she did not smile, she did something more than smile, for her face shone just as the Moon-Angel's face shone when he looked at the bright star that beamed red and blue—as though a bright light were behind the face, and turned to a translucent rosy red. If you want to see how it looked, just hold your hand up before a strong light, and see how the rosy brightness shines through your fingers.

One day David and Phyllis were walking together down the garden path. There were rose bushes all around, and the bright warm air was full of the smell of flowers, and the trees over their heads were full of pink and white blossoms. Beside the blossoms, there were many fruit, purple plums, rosy apples, pears as yellow as pure gold. David and Phyllis were walking hand in hand, and they were very quiet. The other children were playing over on the lawn beyond the rose bushes, and they two could hear them shouting and laughing. Over across the trees they could see the tall, steep roof of the red brick house. Above that, again, was the tall tower, and the round clock face, and the brass weather-cock, that shone like a spark of yellow fire as the breeze blew it this way and that.

"I shall have to go back again pretty soon," said David.

"Go where?" said Phyllis.

"Back into the moon," said David.

"I thought you had come to live with us all the time," said Phyllis.

"No; I am not," said David. "I am only out for a holiday until the Moon-Angel sends for me to come back again."

"And does the Moon-Angel live in the moon-house?" asked Phyllis.

"No; but he comes there for three days in every month," said David.

"What does he come for?"

"He comes to look at the star that shines red and blue."

"What does he look at the star for?"

David stopped to think—and he could not tell. When he had not tried to think about it, it seemed to him that he knew why the Moon-Angel looked at the star, but when he tried to think he knew nothing.

Yes; that is the way with all of us—when we try to think about it, then we cannot tell; when we do not try to think about it, then we know all about it. "I don't know why he looks at the star," said David. "Only he says that he is making old things new again."

"What kind of old things does he make new again?" asked Phyllis.

"That I do not know," said David.

"But why do you have to go back into the moon again?" said Phyllis.

"Because the Man-in-the-moon will gather in the stars again, and then I'll have to polish them with lamb's wool," said David.

"And were they always polished that way?"

"Yes."

"But who was it polished them before you went into the moon?" said Phyllis.

Again David stopped to think, and then he couldn't tell that either. It seemed to him that he did know until he thought about it, and then he knew nothing. "I don't know," said he, and then—"Will you be sorry when I have gone back into the moon?"

"Yes; I will," said Phyllis.

"When I grow up," said David, "and when you grow up, then we will be married."

Phyllis turned her face, and looked at David, and he looked at her. As he did so, he felt a strange and wonderful thrill at his heart, such as he never felt before. It was so keen that it hurt him, and so sweet that it made his breast ache. He did not know what it was.

"Yes," she whispered, "we shall be married." Then suddenly she snatched her hand away from his and ran away, laughing like a peal of silver bells. The next moment she was gone around the bushes and was with the other children again.

David stood for a while and wondered why his heart fluttered so. Then he followed after her, and he felt very sheepish and ashamed. When he came back to the other children she would not look at him or pay any attention to him. David felt hurt that she should act so. He did not know that she acted in that way because she was a little girl. That is the way little girls always act—and big girls too. Why they do so, nobody but the Moon-Angel knows.

Tinkle-tinkle-tinkle! It was that same afternoon, and David heard the bell ringing. He was playing with all his might and main, but he stopped and stood still, for he knew that the bell was ringing for him. Sure enough, there was the moon-house, and there was the open door and the back stairs, and there stood the Man-in-the-moon in the doorway, ringing the bell, just as a teacher rings the bell when play-time is over.

"Must I really go?" said David to the beautiful lady.

"Yes; you must go," said the beautiful lady.

David ran to her and flung his arms around her; she stooped over and kissed him. "Hurry," said she, "or it will be too late."

"Good by! Good by!" cried David, as he ran away toward the moon-house.

"Good by! Good by!" called the children after him. "Come back soon, again."

"I will if I can," called David over his shoulder.

The Man-in-the-moon reached out his hand. David took it, and stepped up into the door. Click-clack! and then he was inside of the moon, once more.

He went up stairs to the second story. The Moon-Angel

had gone. One of the windows was open, and there was a tiny thread of white light shining on the side of the moon-house.

By and by the folk down in the world would look up and say, "Yonder is the new moon."

IX

The Last Play-Day

*D*AY after day the moon grew brighter and brighter, and at last it was full again.

Every day David looked out of one of the second story windows, and every day he saw something new.

One day, what should he see but the moon-path itself stretching across the water far away into the distance. At the end of it were dark rocks against the sky. David knew very well what place it was now. It was the place whence he had started upon his journey for the moon. There was the flat rock with the waves beating up against it. He could even see the roofs of the village; and—yes—who should that be but Hans Krout himself sitting on the rocks. Hans was looking out across the moon-path toward the moon. He saw David almost as soon as David had seen him, and he waved his hand toward him. "How goes it, David?" he called across the water.

"It goes well," called David in answer.

"Going to take another trip?" said Hans Krout.

"Yes," said David; "good bye!" Then the moon rose up above the edge of the water, and Hans Krout and the rocks and the distant roofs of the village and the moon-path all faded slowly, slowly away. "Good bye!" called Hans Krout's voice, now faint in the distance, across the water. Then all was gone, and nothing was there except the empty sky and the bright stars, while the moon floated up into the hollow space like a big round bubble. Then David knew that he could go back home again whenever he chose. It made him feel very happy, for, strange as it may sound, no one cares to live in the moon-house forever, wonderful as it all is. Either one wants after a while to get back home again, or else one wants to get out the back door into the moon-garden, or somewhere else.

So once more David lived in the moon-house while it waned and waned, and as it floated in the hollow-sky he polished and polished the stars with lamb's-wool till they shone and sparkled brighter than ever. When the moon was full, the basket was full of stars; as it waned there were fewer and fewer in the basket, until all were gone. Then again the moon-light was gone, and the second-story window-shutters were all shut, and everything was dark.

Once more David sat down in the moon-kitchen with the Man-in-the-moon, watching him mend and stitch, and patch and cobble, and tinker and cook and make the beds, and now and then read the almanac by candle-light. But all the time David was watching the Man-in-the-moon he was also watching the stairway into the second story and the door that opened into it as well; for he knew that the Moon-Angel would come again as he had come before, and he was waiting for him.

Suddenly, one morning, he was there again—the Moon-Angel. David heard the singing and saw the light, and he knew the Moon-Angel was there. This time, without waiting for the Man-in-the-moon to tell him to do so, he ran up-stairs to the second story and opened the door. There was the Moon-Angel gazing at the star. It flickered and blazed and shone now red, now blue, while the two stars in the Moon-Angel's eyes flickered and blazed and shone now red and now blue as did the star. The Moon-Angel smiled a smile, and he looked at David without ceasing to look at the star.

"What is it, David?" said the Moon-Angel; "do you wish to go back to the moon-garden again?"

"Yes," said David, "if I can be spared."

"You shall go," said the Moon-Angel, "for three days."

"Down the back stairs?" said David.

"Down the back stairs," said the Moon-Angel.

David looked around, and there were the back stairs. Who then so happy as he? He scampered away down the back stairs, and this time he knew them so well that he did not have to feel his way. Down he ran and down he ran, and there was the sunlight shining through the cracks of the door. Again he heard the voices of children upon the other side of the door. Click-clack! He lifted the latch, and there he was out in the dazzling sunlight once more.

The voices of the children stopped the moment he stepped out of the moon. "Oh-h-h-h!" cried all the children, "here is David again." The beautiful lady was sitting on the soft, warm grass, holding in her lap a new little child, who had just come into the moon-garden. He sat with his thumb in his mouth, staring at David with his big, round, blue eyes. Then all the children ran to David and began hugging and kissing him—that is, all of them except Phyllis. She stood a little way off, looking at David with her finger in her mouth. The beautiful lady looked at him too, and smiled until her face shone.

*   *   *   *   *

Thus it was for five months. During that time David lived in the moon and did his work and looked out of the windows, and for three days in every month he went into the moon-garden and played with the children. And it seemed to him that that was what he lived for—to play those three days in the moon-garden.

Then one time the beautiful lady took him by the hand and led him into the house. He went with her, wondering. She led him along a passage-way until they came to her own room, which was at the far end of the long house. It was a pretty room, that looked out into the garden through tall clear windows with thin curtains, and everything in it was sky-blue. There was the lady's desk and her pens and ink and account book. David looked about him, wondering why she had brought him there.

She laid her hand upon David's shoulder and spoke to him. "This is the last time you can come into the moon-garden, David," said she.

David looked at her like one struck dumb. At first he did not understand her words; when he did, it seemed to him as though everything was falling away from him. Then he felt his throat begin to choke and choke. Was it then true? Was he never to come back to the beautiful moon-garden again; never to see Phyllis again; never to play with the children again?

"No," said the beautiful lady, just as if he had spoken, "you are never to come back into the moon-garden again."

"Why not?" said David.

"Because," said she, "before this time next month you will be twelve years old, and no one can live here after he or she is twelve years old."

"Why not?" said David.

The beautiful lady smiled in answer. "Ah, David," said she, "many ask that question, but only one can answer it— that one is the Moon-Angel himself. Yes, David, it seems to be sad that we cannot always be happy like little children; but so it is, David. Innocent little children must grow into men and women who are not innocent. Why it should be so only the Moon-Angel can tell. Nevertheless, so it is, and as it is with others down in the brown world, so it must be with you here, David. For the time has now come when you must leave us here, so that you may grow up into a man, and thus be able to do the work for which you were sent."

"But I would rather live in the moon-garden and be happy," said David.

Again the lady smiled until her face shone bright as the Moon-Angel's face shone when he smiled. "Aye," said she, "so it is with all of us, David. We would all like to be happy, but it cannot be so. You must leave the moon-garden now, and must go away and grow to be a man."

David stood silent, thinking about it. "And am I never to see Phyllis again?" said he at last, almost crying.

"I did not say you were never to see Phyllis again," said the lady. "That depends upon yourself." She looked at David in the eyes. "Tell me," said she, "what did you say to Phyllis one day? Did you not say that you two should be married when you grew up?"

"Yes," said David, and he blushed fiery red.

"Then if it is to be so, you must do something to win her," said the lady. "For, listen, David, Phyllis is not as other children. You did not know it, and she does not know it; but she is a Princess, and her father is a great King."

"A Princess!" cried out David.

"Yes," said the lady, "a Princess."

Poor David stood staring at her. "Then she will not think of me when she grows up," said he. "She will forget me."

"That remains to be seen," said the lady. "She will not forget you if you do the work for which you were sent."

"And what work is that?" said David.

"It is," said the lady, "to find the Wonder-Box and the Know-All Book, which lies in the Iron Castle of the Iron Man, and to bring it back to the brown earth again. That is what you were really sent here to do."

"And how am I to do all that?" said David. "How am I to find the Wonder-Box and the Know-All Book and the Iron Castle of the Iron Man? I never heard tell of them before."

"I will tell you," said the lady. "First of all you are to go around behind the Moon-Angel."

"That is not much to do," said David.

"Is it not?" said the lady. "Ah, David, you do not know what you say. He who can dare to do that, can dare anything."

"I don't understand you," said David.

"Don't you? But you will after you have tried. Just now you must listen to what I have to say, for the time draws near when you must go. If, when it comes to doing it, you dare to go behind the Moon-Angel to the Moon-ocean, where the great gray cliffs of rocks look down on the sea, and where the old woman with the red petticoat lives, then she will tell you what to do."

"And who is the old woman with the red petticoat?" said David.

"Ah, David," said the lady, "even I cannot tell you that. Few have seen her, and fewer still have talked with her. But this I know: she can tell you all about the Wonder-Box and the Know-All Book, and what you are to do to find them. For she knows everything, and more beside."

"Then I will go to her," said David.

The lady smiled. "Do so," said she. "But first you will have to go beyond and behind the Moon-Angel."

"I can easily do that," said David again. "I am not afraid of the Moon-Angel." Again the lady smiled, and this time, oh, so strangely, for she knew what it was to go behind the Moon-Angel. David did not know; but she knew, and she looked almost with pity on him as she smoothed the hair back from his forehead. "God bless you, David," said she. "But hark! there is the bell."

Tinkle-tinkle-tinkle! Yes; there was the bell, and there was the moon-house, and there was the Man-in-the-moon standing, ringing the bell just as the school teacher rings the bell when playtime is over.

"May I not say good-bye to the other children?" said David.

"No," said the lady; "I will say good-by for you."

"May I not even say good-bye to Phyllis?"

"No; not even to her."

Tinkle-tinkle-tinkle! sounded the bell again.

"Then I will say good-bye to you," said poor little David, in a choked voice, and he flung his arms around the lady's neck. She pressed him close, close to her, and kissed him upon the forehead. "Good-bye," said she. Then she put him from her, and he turned and ran away, the big, round moon, the garden and all blurring to the hot tears that brimmed his eyes.

The Man-in-the-moon reached down his hand, and David

took it. "A long step," said the Man-in-the-moon. That is it." Click-clack! And there was David inside the moon again, with the back door shut upon all that he had left behind.

X

Behind the Moon-Angel

*T*o get behind the Moon-Angel. Ah! little child, that is the thing of all things to do. And yet if you could get there, it would only be to see things turned topsyturvy. That is all—to see things turned topsyturvy. And yet everybody in the world is trying, and working, and praying, and longing to get behind the Moon-Angel, or at least to see a glimpse of what is behind him. Few, few, there are who really get behind him; few there are who even so much as see behind him. I have heard people say, "Oh, if I could only just once see ever so little of what is behind the Moon-Angel, then I would be satisfied, for then, maybe, I should see for myself those wonderful things that are there and which many folk talk about and some believe in." That is what I have heard people say. Maybe they would be satisfied if they saw those things, and maybe they would not, but, whether they would or would not, they do not often see what they want to see—perhaps because they try so hard to see it.

Now I will tell you something:—I saw behind the Moon-Angel once—just a little peep. I do not know how it happened, but so it was. I was not really behind the Moon-Angel, you understand, I only just had a glimpse of what was behind him. It was by the seashore and back of the sand-hills, and the sun shone hot—as hot as fire—and the-sea gulls flew over my head, and the dry grass hissed and whispered in the hot wind that blew across the quivering sands. I could hear the breakers far away—Boom! boom!—but I could not see the ocean. Then suddenly I saw the Moon-Angel come walking across the sand. He went past me, and then I saw behind him. What did I see? Oh, I wish I could tell you. But when I try to remember what I saw, then I forget all about it. All I know is that ever since then I have seen things turned topsyturvy, and men walk on their heads instead of their heels, and trees grow upside down, and that I hear wise men talk nonsense.

However, all this is neither here nor there, nor t'other place, and if I stop to speak of such things, I shall never be able to tell you the story of David,—and that story is ever so much more worth the telling. Yes; for David knew more in his little finger about the Moon-Angel and what was behind him than I shall ever be able to learn with my whole body—at least until I have cracked through the crust of things and got back into the Land of Right-side-up again.

Well, for a month of days David did his work, and rubbed the stars and rubbed the stars, and they never shone as brightly as they did in that time. The moon waxed and waxed, and then it waned and waned, until all was dark about the moon-house and all the shutters shut again.

David sat in the moon-kitchen, and waited and waited, and, by and by, there was the light under the door up stairs, and he knew that the Moon-Angel had come again. David ran up stairs and opened the door, and there was the Moon-Angel.

But now he was not standing looking out of the window at the star that shone first red and then blue, and flickered and blazed, and then shone red and then blue again; he was standing in the middle of the room and was looking straight at David.

And how shall I tell you what David saw and what he did? How shall any one tell it? It was all so strange, so strange that it does not fit easily into the words of A B C's, and when a body begins telling it, it breaks all into a jumble and sounds like a fairy-tale, that is not real.

When David saw the Moon-Angel he stopped short, and stood still and as though turned to stone. He had never seen the Moon-Angel look as he looked now, and the little boy was filled with awe. For now the Moon-Angel's face shone like white light, and across his breast was a word of five letters, the letters like forms of fire. No wonder little David stood as though turned to stone. For, oh! little child, the Moon-Angel is terrible, terrible when you see him thus.

"David," said the Moon-Angel, "David, I am waiting for you to come to me, and to pass beyond me."

But for the first time David was frightened at the Moon-Angel.

"Oh, I am afraid! I am afraid!" said he.

"David, David," said the Angel, "why are you afraid?"

"I do not know," said David; "but I am afraid—I am afraid of you!"

Until now the moon-house and the moon-garden had seemed to David to be like a beautiful dream. Now, in his newborn fear, it was as though everything had suddenly changed; as though even they—the moon and the garden— had changed to a dream in which there was something of terror and darkness.

"Will you not come to me?" said the Moon-Angel, and when he spoke thus David could not refuse.

Slowly, slowly he went forward to meet the Moon-Angel. The Moon-Angel opened his arms and took David into them.

* * * * *

What had happened? Was it a dream? David found himself standing alone. At first it was cold—oh, so cold—and all around was a blank whiteness as of a drifting storm of snow. It grew colder and colder; the icy wind seemed to strike into the marrow of his bones, and he went forward staggering as through deep snow. Presently it seemed to him that he could not bear the cold any longer. But it did not last for long. Just as he began to feel that he could no longer endure the freezing cold, it began to pass away.

Then presently he felt that the air was beginning to grow mild and tepid. The icy wind had ceased to blow, and it grew warmer and warmer. In a little while the chill air had become mild and balmy. All around David was still a blank whiteness, only now it was the whiteness, not of snow, but of a silvery mist that hid everything from his sight. He could see nothing; but it seemed to him that he could hear from beyond the veil of mist the sounds of flowing waters and of rustling leaves; that he could smell the odor of flowers; that he could hear the song of birds, and far away a faint music as of piping and the echo as of distant voices talking and laughing together. All this he seemed to hear faintly and distantly, but he could see nothing for the misty whiteness all around him. This, too, lasted only for a little while, and then it also began to change.

For presently it began to grow warmer and still warmer. Then it grew hotter and still hotter. The silver mist began to fade and melt and by and by to change to a vapor of fiery copper. Then instead of these other sounds of leaves and birds and voices, which also dimmed away into silence, there came nearer and still nearer a crackling as of flames. David knew that fire lay before him; that if he went on he must pass through it. Should he turn back? No. He felt that he was every instant becoming stronger and stronger to bear the fiery trials. He did not know that he was growing into a man; that it was not moments that were passing, but years of time. Then he was in the midst of the fire. Oh, how hot it was! His brain swam dizzily, and he did not seem to feel the ground beneath his feet. He was gasping for breath, and crackling sparks of fire seemed to dance before his eyes. A step or two more, and he knew that he must fall, and what would become of him then? He wondered how he was able to bear it.

Suddenly an iron door stood before him, and he knew that thence he might escape. He flung himself against it, but it did not open. It was burning hot to his hands, but he felt and found the latch. He pushed it, and then the door swung open, and he fell headlong out upon the ground beyond.

It was over. It was done. He had passed beyond the Moon-Angel, and so much of his labor was over. He lay there upon the ground gasping and panting. A cool, moist breeze played around him, and seemed to bathe him with a balm of comfort. Then it began to come to him that he was upon the rocky shore of the sea. The thunder of the breakers and the rattling hiss of the receding waters, the rushing of the wind, and the clamoring of the sea-gulls, filled his ears with sound.

He lay there upon the cool, damp stones, motionless, panting, but quiet and at peace. But he was no longer a little boy; he was a grown man.

Yes; he thought that he had been only a few minutes in passing beyond the Moon-Angel; but it had really been ten years, and in that time he had grown from a child into a man.

Few there are who grow to manhood thus, little child. Do you not understand? No? Perhaps some day you will— perhaps, perhaps.

XI

The Land of Nowhere

BY and by David arose and stood upon his feet. Then he looked down at himself and saw as with a sudden shock of wonder that he had grown into a man. He could not believe it at first. What wonder! What delight!—a great tall man with strong limbs and a big body. He swung his arms and felt their strength; he filled out his chest, breathing in great volumes of the cool, salt air. He felt strong to do anything. He *was* strong to do anything, for he had passed through frost and fire and beyond the Moon-Angel, and he who has done that can do anything.

Then he looked around him. On one side was the ocean,

on the other side rose beetling cliffs that towered high, high into the air, the summit swimming dizzily against the blue sky and the floating clouds. High aloft against the face of the cliffs flicked and fluttered the white wings of the sea-gulls, and their clamor sounded incessantly through the ceaseless thunder and crash of the breakers.

Away on the top of the cliff, some distance beyond where he stood, he could just see the roof of a cottage, and the red chimney, from which the blue smoke drifted away into the air. In front of the cottage was a woman with a red petticoat that flamed like a spark of fire against the blue sky. She was hanging out clothes upon a line, but David knew that that must be the old woman with the red petticoat of whom the lady of the moon-garden had spoken—the old woman who knew everything and more beside.

He went forward along the seashore, the seagulls rising everywhere from the cliffs at his coming, clamoring and screaming with a multitudinous outcry of voices. So with the noise of the sea-gulls dinning in his ears, and the thunder of the breakers filling his soul, David walked forward along the shore until, by and by, he came to a path that led to the face of the cliff, where there was a flight of stone steps built up through the clefts of the crags to the top of the pinnacled rocks. Up these steps he climbed, up and up, the moon-ocean spreading out wider and wider below him the higher he climbed. By and by he was at the top, and he could look out and down upon the crawling, wrinkled water beneath him, stretching away as boundless and empty as nothing at all. There was not a boat or a sail in sight, but only far away the long line of horizon, and from that the pearly sky that arched up into a deep blue dome overhead. Below him flicked and flitted the sea-gulls about the rocky face of the cliff, their screaming clamor coming up to him commingled with the ceaseless noise of the distant waters.

Then he turned around, and there was the cottage a little distance away. The old woman with the red petticoat had gone back into the house, but the clothes were hanging on the line, snowy white and fluttering in the wind.

Then David saw what they were.

They were the souls of men.

From the outside they looked only like linen clothes, but David was able now to see things from the inside, and so could see that *they were the souls of men*.

Aye, aye; this is true, little child. That dear old woman who lives up on the cliff in the Land of Nowhere—that dear old woman with the red petticoat—that is what she does. Day after day, day after day, she washes white the souls of men, and hangs them out in the sun and the sweet warm air to dry. She has been doing so ever since the beginning of time; ever since the moment that the first baby came into the world and lifted up its voice and cried. Ever since then she has been washing, washing, washing the souls of men, which grow so soiled by use that after a while they would become unfit to wear if it were not for that dear old woman upon the cliff, who washes them until they are as white as snow, and then hangs them out in the sun to dry.

David went up to the door, but before he could knock the old woman called out to him to come in, and in he went.

"Are you hungry?" said she.

"Yes; I am," said David.

"Then you must eat something," said she, "for no man can do his best work unless he eats."

So David sat down to the table, and the old woman brought him a bowl of milk and a piece of bread. David did not know how hungry he was until he began eating. Then it seemed to him he could not eat enough. He ate and ate and ate, and as he ate, he looked across the table at the old woman, who sat with her hands folded, looking placidly back at him. He thought he had never seen such a sweet, lovable face in all his life before. Her hair was as white as snow, and was brushed back under a cap that was still whiter than that. Her face was covered all over with wrinkles, so close and so fine that it made David think of the Man-in-the-moon.

So David looked at her as he ate his bread and drank his milk, and when he had ended his meal he pushed back his bowl and spoon, and looked at her again and yet again. She smiled. "Well," said she; "and what do you think of me?"

"I think you are very beautiful," said David.

The old woman laughed. "Do you?" said she. "Most men think I am very ugly. And so you have come from the other side of the Moon-Angel to find the Wonder-Box and the Know-All Book to take them back to the brown earth, where they belong, have you?"

"Yes," said David; "that is what I have come to do, if you will tell me how I am to do it."

"If I will tell you?" said the old woman of the cliff. "Why else am I here except to tell you that? Why, David, lad, that is why I live here. But have you had enough to eat?"

"Yes, I have," said David.

"That is good; for he must not go hungry who has such work to do as lies before you."

"But, first of all, tell me," said David, "what is this Wonder-Box, and what is the Know-All Book? And why am I to take them back to the brown earth again?"

"Am I to tell you the whole story?" said the old woman of the cliff, "the whole story?"

"Yes," said David, "the whole story."

"Very well," said the old woman. And so she did, and this was how she told

The Story of the Know-All Book.

Once in that far-away beginning of time when everything was young and innocent, and the sky was fresh, and the sunshine new, and there was no such thing as sadness and sorrow (or joy and delight, for the matter of that), there was a woman and a man who lived like innocent little children in a beautiful garden of paradise.

"That was Adam and Eve," said David.

"No," said the old woman of the cliff; "it was Eve and Adam."

"And what is the difference?" said David.

"What is the difference when you say 'the light grows dim,' instead of saying 'the dim grows light'?" said the old woman.

"I don't know," said David.

"I do," said the old woman.

And this garden of paradise was a beautiful, beautiful place, with soft green grass shaded by trees that bore blossoms and fruit at the same time; where sweet birds sang from morning to night, and all was innocence and peace.

"That was like the moon-garden," said David.

"Aye," said the old woman. "It *was* the moon-garden, too."

Well, one time a man came walking into this garden where the innocent woman and innocent man lived. The two saw him coming among the trees and the blossoms— a tall, stately figure dressed in a long gray robe that sparkled all over with dim stars.

"That was like the Moon-Angel," said David.

"It *was* the Moon-Angel," said the old woman.

Under his arm the man carried a box of iron, shut and locked, but with a golden key in the keyhole. "Children," said he, "here is a box for you to keep. In it is the greatest joy and the greatest sorrow in the world. Keep it closed, and you will always be happy as you now are. But if you open it, sorrow will come upon you." Then he went away, leaving the box behind him. Seven days passed, and then one day the woman said to the man, "I wonder what there can be in that box? The tall man said that in it was the greatest joy in the world." "He said that the greatest sorrow of the world was in it also," said the man. "But," said the woman, "if we open it we will behold the greatest joy in the world." "And we will let the greatest sorrow out into the world," said the man.

"Now, what would you have done, David?" said the old woman of the cliff.

David spoke up boldly (you must remember he was a man now). "I would have opened the box," said he, "for surely it is worth suffering the greatest sorrow for the sake of the greatest joy."

The old woman smiled. "Ah, David," said she, "you say that because you have passed through the ice and the fire, and out beyond the Moon-Angel. But what you say is true enough; it *is* worth suffering the greatest sorrow for the sake of the greatest joy. That was why the Moon-Angel brought the iron box to the man and the woman—it was the Wonder-Box, David."

"And the Know-All Book was the greatest joy?" said David.

"Yes," said the old woman.

"And the man opened it?" said David.

"Yes," said the old woman.

The man turned the golden key in the lock of the box, and as he did so he shivered and trembled. The birds had ceased to sing, the leaves had ceased to rustle in the breezes, and the air hung as silent as death; the sky became overcast as with a thin sheet of cloud, and there was a sound as of distant thunder. "Open the box!" cried the woman in a piercing voice, and then the man lifted the lid.

Instantly it flew back wide open, and out belched a great cloud of terror like a great volume of smoke. It rose higher and higher into the air above the tops of the trees, spreading out wide into a huge dark cloud. The man and the woman clung together, trembling with terror. Then they saw that the smoke was beginning to form itself into the image of a man, and then the two turned and ran away through the garden.

"But did they then not see the joy that was within the Wonder-Box?" said David.

The old woman shook her head. "No, David," said she, "few there are who pause to see the joy that lies behind when black sorrow stands between."

The man and the woman fled away through the garden. All about them was that darkness of terror, for the sky was overcast with gloom, and Sorrow was coming fast after them. On it came through the trees, scattering fruit and flowers, rending and tearing. On and on sped the man and the woman, until at last they suddenly came to an iron door that was shut against them. The man leaped forward and pressed the latch. The door flew open, and the two ran out into the world beyond. They stood upon a shingled beach, with the ocean stretching away before them. But Sorrow had followed after them, and Joy was left behind in the iron-box.

"And what happened then?" said David.

"I will tell you," said the old woman.

The two wandered along the shore for a long, long distance, until they came at last to a country where men lived.

There was no king and no queen to that country, and as this man and woman stood head and shoulders taller than the men and women of the common world, and as they were so fair and beautiful, and because their faces shone as with white light, the people of the city took them for their king and queen.

By and by the two died, and their son became king. Then he died and his son was king. Then he died and his son was king, and so on for generations and generations.

But the Wonder-Box and the Know-All Book were lost. And the garden stood utterly deserted.

For after the man and the woman had fled, there came one day the dreadful Iron Man of the Iron Castle, before whose face even the little birds fled away. He found the Box and the Book lying under a tree and took them away with him; and from that time the eyes of man have never seen them again. But nevertheless this was known: that some day—aye, some day—a hero would appear who would bring back the Wonder-Box to the earth. That time there should be a princess, and after the hero had found the Wonder-Box and the Know-All Book and had brought them back to the earth again, he should marry her, and by and by should himself be king over that land.

And this, little child, is the story of the Wonder-Box and the Know-All Book.

And is it true? True? Aye, it *is* true. At least it was true one time, and thanks to great A and little izzard it will be true again sometime to come.

* * *

But David sat motionlessly gazing at the wrinkled face of the old woman, and his eyes shone and his cheeks burned like fire. It had come into his mind to wonder if it could be possible that he was to be the hero who should bring back the Wonder-Box to the brown earth again? could it be possible? He did not dare to ask the question, but the old woman answered it without being asked. "Yes, David," said she, and her voice was very, very sweet, "you are the man."

"Then let me go and find it," cried out David.

The old woman laughed. "Patience, David," she said, "patience, patience. Tomorrow morning you shall set out to do your work. Tonight you must sleep, and rest yourself. But, tell me, how will you set about to find the Iron Castle of the Iron Man?"

"I do not know," said David.

"Then I will tell you," said the old woman. "Tomorrow you shall set foot to the westward. You will journey all day, but toward evening you will come to a rocky desert, and there you will find a fountain of water. Every day the Black Horse who lives in the sky comes to that fountain to drink and to refresh himself. He alone can carry you to the Iron Castle of the Iron Man. Tomorrow, before you leave, I will give you a bridle with a golden bit. If with it you can bridle the Black Horse, then you will have tamed him, and will be his master."

"I wish it were tomorrow," said David.

The old woman laughed again. "Time enough for that, David," said she.

XII

The Black Winged Horse

*T*HE next morning the old woman of the cliff gave to David a bridle studded with silver bosses, and the bit that hung from the bridle was of pure gold. "Take it," she said; "with it alone you can tame the Black Winged Horse."

David took it and thanked her, and then started off upon his way. The day was bright and lovely, and David, turning his face to the westward, strode across the field away from the ocean and inland. The sun had hardly yet arisen, and all the earth was bright and filled with the sparkling sheen of dew, that, in the slanting brightness, turned the spider webs everywhere into little fairy sheets of silver. The few small trees that stood out solitary here and there upon the rolling downs did not move a single leaf, but remained still and motionless in the motionless air. Everywhere the birds were chanting a jubilant melody. The multitudinous song seemed to fill all the air near and afar.

David swelled out his breast, drinking in deep draughts of the sweet morning air as he strode along. He turned and looked back. The old woman of the cliff was standing looking after him, a red petticoat, a gleam of fire in the misty brightness of the morning. He waved his hand toward her, and she waved her hand toward him. Then he turned again and strode away to the far-reaching westward.

He was almost the only man who had ever seen that old woman with the eyes of flesh, and he never saw her again.

But thus it was that David set out upon that journey all in the dewy freshness of the morning, with the song of the birds ringing in his ears, and the fragrance of the early day keen in his nostrils. Yes; and so do we all set forth upon the task that lies before us with buoyant and lusty joyousness of hope filling all the heart.

The day grew fuller and fuller, the sun rose higher and higher, and shone hotter and hotter until it beat down fiercely upon David's head. And now he had left the high and windy downs and all around him lay hot, reeking fenlands with bogs and quags, and here and there a stunted pollard willow. Now there was no song of birds, but only now and then the deep bull-like bassoon of a great frog hidden under the bank amid the rushes and the arrow-heads. Now and then a heron arose and flapped away in slow and heavy flight. The sweat ran down David's face in streams, and ever and anon he lifted his hat and wiped the trickling drops away with his sleeve.

So it was that he plodded along his way across the oozy fenland, with the hot sun beating down upon him. So do we all toil upon our task when maybe it is half-way done.

The sun began to slant down into the western sky, and now it shone full in his face. He had eaten his noon-day bread, but he was parched with thirst. For now he had left even the fenlands behind, and was walking across a wide and boundless stretch of rocks and boulders and round stones. All was silent, all was dead except now and then when a lizard or a great fat, black cricket would dart across the path from rock to rock. David was very weary, for the round stones slipped and rolled away from under his feet.

So he drew near the end of his journey. So we all of us draw near to the end of our labor, weary, thirsty, stumbling as we go.

The sun was yet two hours high when David, from the top of a naked and rocky hill, saw the fountain of crystal water lying, a bright fragment, in the valley beneath him— that wonderful fountain of water whence the great Black Winged Horse drinks every evening, and so refreshes himself before he again takes his flight to those lofty altitudes of the still blue heavens where he forever circles, dips, hovers in airy and ambient brightness.

David, when he saw the fountain, shouted and leaped and ran down the stony hill to where the little pool lay like a fragment of heaven amid the black, lichen-covered rocks.

He plunged his face and hands and arms into the pool, and drank deep draughts of its crystal coolness. It seemed to fill his veins with fresh strength and his soul with a renewed life. Again and again he drank, and then he paused, breathing deep and full.

As he so paused, hanging over the mirror-like surface of the little pool, watching it as its rippled bosom stilled again into its first glassy smoothness, he suddenly saw reflected in the surface of the water a something that seemed to be a great bird hovering with wings outspread, high in the air above him. He looked up, and there against the blue sky overhead, far, far away, he saw, not a bird, but a wonderful winged horse, circling around and around on wide-spread wings in slow, eagle-like flight against the profound upper depths of fathomless sky.

It was the Winged Horse, and David knew that it must now be coming to drink at the fountain, for already the sun was growing red, and falling toward the west in the last hours of day. He caught up the bridle and flung it over his arm, and then drew back and hid himself among the dark lichen-covered rocks.

The Black Horse circled nearer and nearer, and though its body was black, its wings glistened as white as snow. It circled nearer and nearer, sweeping around and around in narrowing flight, until at last it hovered darkly over the spring of water. Then with its wings reaching high and quivering, it settled slowly, slowly to the earth, until it rested as lightly as a feather upon the solid rock beneath its feet. Still it held its wings poised for a moment or two, then folded them rustling across its back. Then it bent its stately head, and began to drink great draughts of water from the fountain.

Then, quick as a flash, David leaped out and upon it, and before the horse could spring away, he had clutched it by the forelock. Then began a mighty struggle between the horse and the man. It was well for David that he himself had first drunk strength from that fountain, for otherwise he never could have kept his hold, and would have been dashed to pieces under those iron hoofs. For the horse struck at him with its hoofs, and beat at him with its glistening pinions. But it could not shake him loose, and he still kept his hold, clinging fast to it. It tried to fly away into the air, but David's weight held it to the earth. Then it tried to thrust him against the rocks, and to crush him between it and them, but David, stooping suddenly forward, slipped the golden bit into its mouth and between its teeth. Then in an instant all was over. The horse stood trembling and quivering, its body covered with foam, and its widespread nostrils as red as blood. It was tamed, and it bowed its head acknowledging its master. Then after a little while it spoke with a voice as plain as that of a Christian man.

"What would you have of me, master?"

"I would have you take me to the Iron Castle of the Iron Man," said David.

"Then mount upon my back, and I will take you thither, master. But woe is me that it must be so, for you are the first man who has ever sat astride of my back."

David laid his hand upon its back and grasped a crop of its mane. Then, with a leap, he sprang upon it.

XIII

The Iron Castle

*T*HE Black Horse struck its feet upon the ground, and spreading its hovering wings, it sped away, skimming along the surface of the earth. It did not rise into the air, for now it could not do so.

That wonderful Black Winged Horse. So it is, little child; for though, when free of curb and bit, he may soar aloft, higher and higher, until he vanishes like a speck into the bosom of heaven, far, far away beyond the keenest sight, yet, when a man sits astride of his back, as David now sat astride of him, he cannot rise high. He may skim along the surface, riding dry-shod, maybe, over the oceans and the rivers of water, but never rising, when so burdened, higher than the height of a man above the ground.

So the Black Horse skimmed and sped away, carrying David upon its back. Away and away, so swiftly that the dark earth seemed to slide away beneath it, and David had to hold his hat to keep it from flying from his head.

The sun sank, and the gray shadows of twilight seemed to rise upward from the earth, and to lie dim and misty in the hollows of the rocks. On and on sped the horse, on and on. The daylight faded and faded, and one bright star shone out keen and clear in the western sky.

"Look," said the Black Horse, "do you see anything yet?"

David shaded his eyes with his hand. "I see," said he, "far, far away, a speck against the sky."

"It is not a speck," said the Black Horse.

On and on it sped, and the red light in the sky melted into a thin gray, and one starry point after another began to prick through the vault of heaven.

"Look," said the horse, "what do you see by now?"

Again David looked, striving to pierce the distance. "I see," said he, "something against the sky, and it looks like a house, far, far away."

"Aye," said the Black Horse, "it is a house indeed!"

On and on sped the horse, and now the slow moon rose up red and round into the eastern sky. "Tell me," said the horse at last, "what do you see now?"

This time David did not have to look before he spoke. "I see," said he, "a great castle towering as black as ink against the sky, and it is all built of iron—a great dark, grim place, with the iron doors studded all over with bolts, and high up under the eaves a double row of windows with iron gratings shutting them in."

"That," said the Black Horse, "is the Iron Castle of the Iron Man." And as it spoke, it stood at the castle gateway, and David leaped to the ground.

"Whistle when you want me again," said the horse, "and I shall be here." Then instantly it was gone, and David stood all alone, with nothing in front of him but the castle wall and the great door studded all over with iron bolts.

It took the Winged Horse three hours to make that journey from the fountain to the Iron Castle: it would have taken you a life-time—or David either, for the matter of that, hero though he was.

XIV

The Iron Man

*D*AVID looked up at the huge iron door. It was shut and locked.

Beside the doorway a great iron horn hung by a long iron chain from the wall. Over the horn were these words written in letters of red:

> "Whatever man would enter here,
> Must blow a blast both loud and clear."

David set the horn to his lips and blew a blast so loud and long that it rang back again from the dark high walls and under the eaves and made his ears hum. Instantly there was a rumbling and a grumbling as though of distant thunder. The iron bolts within shot grating back and the huge iron door opened slowly, slowly, until it stood open wide. David entered, looking about him wondering.

It was a great, dark, empty room. The risen moon was now shining in at the grated windows, high overhead, and David could see above him a vast vaulted ceiling of iron, and under foot a pavement of iron. Everywhere were dust and cobwebs. Bats and owls were flying silently about in the gloom above. The white moonlight falling aslant upon the walls showed thereon figures of knights and ladies and dragons and giants painted in red. Beyond this great gloomy room was another just like it, and beyond that another and another, until David began to think that there was no end to them. He went on and on, until by and by he saw in the distance a dull glow of red light, and heard the sound of some one moving and the rattle of pans and dishes. He followed the sound until he came to a door. He pushed it open, and there was a room that looked like a great kitchen. In this room was nobody but an old woman and a black cat and a bright fire burning on the hearth. A huge table was spread for supper; on it was a pitcher of ale as big as a barrel, and a goblet as big as a bucket. There was a pewter plate as wide as a cart-wheel, a fork like a pitch fork, and a knife like a scythe. The old woman was busy roasting a whole sheep at the fire. She held a ladle in her hand, with which she basted the roast as she turned it before the blaze. Hearing the door open, she turned and then she saw David standing. Down fell the ladle clattering upon the floor.

She stood staring and staring while David stood gazing back at her. "Who are you?" said the old woman at last, "and whence come you?"

"I am a Christian soul, mother," said David, "and I come from the brown earth on the other side of the moon."

"And what do you seek?" said the old woman.

"I come," said David, "to find the Wonder-Box and the Know-All Book, and to take them back again to the brown earth, where they belong."

"Alas!" said the old woman, "I am sorry for you, for, though you look like a hero rather than like a man, woe to you if the Iron Man comes and finds you here."

"And who are you, mother?" said David.

"I do not know," said the old woman, "except that I am a woman of flesh and blood. I have been here for so long that I have forgotten everything else. But I too am of flesh and blood—that much I do remember."

"Then, if you are really of flesh and blood, you will help me, will you not, mother?" said David.

"I will do what I can, for the sake of flesh and blood," said the old woman. "But hark!" she cried, suddenly, and she put her hand to her ear—"Hark! I hear him coming now!"

David listened, and then he also heard far away a sound of clashing and clattering and clanking and jingling, as of moving iron. He knew that it must be the coming of the

Iron Man, and though his heart beat fast he squared his shoulders to meet the giant.

But the old woman ran to him and caught him by the arm. "Quick!" she cried. "Here!" and she lifted up the lid of a great chest that stood in the corner.

David climbed into the chest, and the old woman shut the lid, leaving him lying in the dust and darkness. Jingle! clink! crash! bang! then the door opened, and in came the Iron Man, breathing fire and smoke out of his iron nostrils. David lifted the lid of the chest a little and saw him as he came.

The Iron Man went to the fire and took up the sheep, spit and all. He laid it upon the great plate on the table and cut it up as one would cut up a partridge. Then he sat down to the table and began to eat and drink, carving the meat with the iron knife as long as a scythe, and thrusting it into his mouth with the fork as large as a pitch fork, and drinking great draughts of ale out of the huge goblet. The ale hissed and sputtered as it went down his iron throat, and a white cloud of steam came out of his nostrils. Nothing was heard for a while but the clash and clatter of knife and fork and the champing and champing of the iron jaws of the Iron Man. All this David saw as he looked out from under the lid of the chest. The Iron Man was thrusting food into his mouth as one might put coal into the mouth of a furnace.

At last the meal was ended, and the Iron Man drew his chair up in front of the fire. "Here," said he to the old woman, "take this key and bring me the Wonder-Box and the Know-All Book. Maybe I can read the book tonight."

Then David, as he peered out from the chest, saw the old woman take the iron key and go to another great iron chest at the further side of the room. She opened the chest and brought out a box of burnished iron that gleamed red in the red fire-light. The box was locked with a golden key, and from the key there hung a fine golden chain. The old woman brought the box to the Iron Man, who opened it with the golden key, and took out a book as white as snow. It was the Know-All Book; the wonder of wonders! Yes; the Know-All Book, which alone could bring the joy of true happiness into the world, whence it had fled when those two—the man and the woman—fled from out the Garden of Paradise.

David watched the Iron Man as he held the book, and looked and looked at it, and tried to read it. He was holding it upside down, the poor giant, for he could not read a single word of it—that wonderful, wonderful book. Ever since that far beginning of time he has been trying to read it, and he is trying to read it still. But he cannot, for between him and it there hangs a veil that only the living soul can pierce to read those words within.

So there he sat now, the poor, blundering giant of smoking fire and hot iron—there he sat, patiently trying and trying to read what was there written, while his eyelids grew heavier and heavier, until by and by he fell asleep. After a while he began to snore, and after another while the book slipped from out his hand and fell to the floor, where it lay—the precious Know-All Book—face downward and forgotten.

Then after a while the old woman came to the chest where David lay hidden. "Now is your time," said she, "if you are man enough to do what you came for."

"I am man enough," said David. "Thank you, mother."

"Ah!" she said, "do not thank me yet, man of flesh and blood, for your trouble is not yet over. But there is the book, and there is the box. Take them if you want them, and get you away if you can."

The Iron Man never moved or stirred, but slept on and on as David picked up the book and put it into the Wonder-Box, shut the lid, locked it, and took the key out of the lock, hanging the golden chain about his neck. There was a handle in the lid of the box; he lifted it and carried it out of the room, and still the Iron Man never stirred, but slept on and on. David went out of the room into the room beyond. The moon had risen high, and great barred patches of square light fell from the windows upon the iron floor beneath. In the vaulted spaces above, all was darkness and stillness. He hurried onward into the next room lit with moonlight, dark and still in the vault above. Beyond that was still another room, and so on and on, until he could not tell where he was. So he went from room to room, and around and around, and on and on, until he knew that he was lost in the vast dark spaces of the Iron Castle. But at last he smelt the night air in the distance, as though it came in at an open door. He ran across the squares of silent moonlight toward it. Yes; there at last was the open door, and there was the night sky outside, all milky with the silent moonlight.

"Now I am safe," thought David.

He did not know what was yet to come.

XV

The Escape

AVID ran toward the open door and freedom.

Out he leaped and down the tall flight of stone steps to the soft earth beneath.

Instantly his foot struck the sod, a sudden and piercing blast of sound burst out upon the silence of the night.

It was the iron horn that hung by the iron chain at the gateway; so sudden and keen was the blast that David stopped short and stood as though rooted to where he stood.

Then in an instant it was as though all the dead and silent castle had sprung awake into life. Lights flashed out; there was an uproar of voices and a clashing and a clattering everywhere. Shutters banged open and doors banged shut. The lights came and went past the windows, and the shadows flew hither and thither across the walls.

And still the iron horn continued to sound its keen and piercing blast.

And now, through the shrill and stunning noise, David could hear another sound—a crashing clank and jingle and the rumbling thunderous tones of a giant voice.

It was the Iron Man, and he was coming.

Then David's wits came back to him like a flash, and he turned to run away.

Suddenly, as he turned to fly, he heard a voice he knew, calling: "Help! Help! Save me! Save me!"

He looked up above, and whom should he see, leaning out of a window close under the eaves, stretching out her arms toward him, but Phyllis.

Yes, Phyllis; but now grown into a beautiful young woman.

What with the noise and the uproar and the wonder of it all, David stood as though bewildered. "Is that you, Phyllis?" he cried.

"Yes; oh, yes!" she called. "Help me—help me away from here!"

"But I thought you were in the moon-garden," cried David.

"So I am," called Phyllis. "This is the moon-garden! Oh, help me away from it!"

Still David stood like one in a maze, not knowing what to do.

The iron horn was still blowing its splitting blast; but through it all the clashing foot-steps of the Iron Man rang ever louder and louder, and nearer and nearer.

And hark! What was that? A bell ringing through all the tumult. David listened, and then he knew what bell it was. It was the Man-in-the-moon ringing his bell at the back door of the moon-house.

"Run, Phyllis," cried David, "up the back stairs, or else we are both lost!"

Then Phyllis's face disappeared from the window up under the eaves, and as David listened he could hear the voice of the Man-in-the-moon, though dull and muffled, speaking to her in the distance just as the old fellow had spoken to him—"Give me your hand—now; a long step—there; that is it." Then came the closing of a door—click!—clack!—and the next minute he heard Phyllis's feet coming running quickly up the back stairs that led from the moon-garden to the second story of the moon-house; nearer—nearer—nearer.—Then suddenly there she was standing beside him, panting from the rapid run.

David caught her by the arm. He could not believe that it was not all a dream until he felt that she was of real flesh and of real blood.

But the Iron Man was coming nearer and nearer. Now again he spoke, and his great voice rumbled and shook within the castle. "Where is he who stole my Wonder-Box and my Know-All Book?" Then the door opened, and out he strode, the fire and smoke rolling out from his nostrils into the still and breathless night.

Phyllis shrieked aloud.

Then David set his fingers to his lips, and blew a shrill, keen whistle.

Instantly, as it had promised, the Black Winged Horse was there, his snow-white pinions glistening in the pallid moonlight. There was not a moment to lose. Quickly David lifted Phyllis to the back of the horse. "To the moon-house!" he cried; and then himself leaped astride of it behind her.

The Iron Man saw them, and he gave a great roar of rage as he came rushing toward them.

Away leaped the horse. Away it sped swifter than the wind, carrying David and Phyllis and the Wonder-Box and the Know-All Book.

"Hold fast!" cried David.

"I will," said Phyllis. Her face was very pale. Her long hair blew back across his breast and face and lips in a soft and silky net.

The golden key still hung by the golden chain about David's neck. It swung from side to side, and every now and then he put his hand up to see if it were safe. He heard the Iron Man shouting and hallooing behind them. He turned and looked over his shoulder to see the smoking and flaming giant coming rushing after them.

Fast flew the Black Winged Horse, skimming like a swallow along the surface of the earth above the rocks and stones, the brambles and briers, but the Iron Man came almost as fast. Now and then he would stop to pick up a huge stone to hurl after them, but on sped the Winged Horse, and then on the Iron Man would come rushing again.

On and on they flew, until at last the darkness of night began to grow gray toward the east, and the daylight grew wider and wider.

Then the sun leaped up round and red out of the east, and once again David turned his head and looked behind him. The Iron Man was still coming rushing after them like a whirlwind. And now the rising sun shone full in his face and turned it as red as blood, and the black smoke from his nostrils trailed away behind, melting and fading into the clear and lucid ether of early morning.

"Look!" said the horse. "But look ahead and not behind. Tell me, what do you see?"

Then David looked, shading his eyes from the level glare of the sun. "I see," said he, "something that shines like a flame of fire away—yes, it is the old woman's cottage upon the cliff, and beyond that I see the far-away edge of the ocean."

"Aye," said the Black Winged Horse, "and there my labor ends. That far I can carry you, but no further. Beyond the brow of the cliff you must go alone."

"But the Iron Man!" cried David.

"Beyond the cliff you must save yourself. I cannot carry you further than that."

"But Phyllis!" cried David again.

"You must save her, too. I cannot carry you further."

"But how shall we escape?" said David.

"You must go in at the door out of which you came. There is no other escape."

"But the fire," said David, "and the ice through which I passed."

"There will neither be fire to burn you any more nor ice to freeze you. He who has passed through them once, shall never have to pass through them again."

"But Phyllis," said David. "How will she pass through the fire and the ice?"

"Neither will they harm her while she is with you," said the Black Winged Horse.

Phyllis had listened to all that they had said; but she did not understand it.

Then David looked behind him again for the last time. The Iron Man was far, far behind.

Then they reached the end of their journey. The Black Winged Horse sped past the old woman's cottage. She was nowhere to be seen, but the white clothes were hanging out upon the line, blowing in the wind. On sped the Black Horse, and to the very edge of the cliff, and then he stopped short. "This is the end," cried he. "I can go no further."

David leaped to the earth, and then lifted Phyllis down from the horse's back.

Far below the breakers were dashing and foaming as white as milk among the rocks and boulders, and all about the face of the cliff, and away out into the empty air, the sea-gulls flew clamoring. But neither Phyllis nor David thought of what they saw. She looked over her shoulder at the looming Giant rushing toward them. "Oh, look!" she cried. "How fast he is coming!"

"But will you not now set me free?" said the horse.

"Yes," said David, "I will. He caught the bridle and loosed the buckle. "Farewell," said he, and as he spoke he stripped the bridle and the bit away.

The Black Horse gave a great neigh like the peal of a trumpet. Clashing his hoofs upon the rocks, he spread his wonderful white wings, and, leaping into the air, flew clapping and thundering away—away—away—now circling and soaring in upward spiral flight, until he became a spot upon the sky—twinkled—was lost—was there—was gone.

XVI

Back to the Moon-House

*B*UT meantime David and Phyllis were running down the stone steps that led from the brow of the cliffs to the seashore below, David carrying the Wonder-Box tightly clasped beneath his arm, and pressing the key to his breast with the other hand. The Iron Man was still coming rushing after them, but David felt sure that they would now escape, for after they had reached the beach below, it was only a little distance to the iron door whence he had come from the other side of the Moon-Angel. He knew that what the Black Horse had said was true—they had but to enter there, and they would be safe.

They reached the beach, and then hurried along the stony shore toward the door, out of which David had come the day before. As they ran, David looked back over his shoulder, and saw that the Iron Man was heavily and cumbersomely climbing down the stone steps from above, his head and shoulders just showing gigantically above the edge of the rocky clefts.

On hurried the two, and there, at last, was the door. David gave a shout of delight, and rushed toward it.

.   .   .   .   .

It was locked.

.   .   .   .   .

David stood as still as a stone. His very heart seemed to cease to beat within him.

Locked! Could it be? He turned again and strove to push it open.

It stood as solid as the rock into which it was built.

"Open the door!" cried Phyllis. "Oh, open the door, David, he is coming."

"I cannot open it," said David, hoarsely. "It is locked."

"Oh, try again," cried Phyllis. "Try again, David."

But David shook his head. "It is locked, Phyllis," said he, dully. "We cannot go in now."

He knew that they were not to enter, and now the Iron Man was coming stumbling among the rocks straight toward them, looming bigger and bigger as he approached.

David set the Wonder-Box down upon the step in front of the door, and then went forward to meet the Iron Giant. He had no weapon with him, nothing with which to fight his battle. He looked about him as he went toward the Giant, and seeing a sharp and jagged stone, he picked it up, weighing it in his hand. He looked back and saw that Phyllis was sitting crouched together in a heap against the door, watching him, and trembling and shuddering. Then he looked around again; the Giant was close to him.

Then the Iron Man stopped short, and stood for a little space looking at David. Suddenly he burst into a great vibrating roar of laughter, a roar that sounded like the stroke of the clapper of a huge bell. "Now you are mine," he said. "And the girl and you shall come back to my Iron Castle to serve me as long as you live." Then he reached out his great iron hand as though to grasp David by the hair.

Then David, swinging his body, hurled, with all his might and main, the great jagged stone he held straight at the head of the Iron Man.

Straight it flew, striking the Iron Man right in the center of the forehead. There was a clanging crash as the stone struck its mark, a tinkle as of broken glass, and, as David looked, he saw for one instant in the center of the Giant's forehead a broken and shattered hole in the hollow iron. For that instant he saw that the Iron Man was all alight within as with red and flaming fire; the next there came a gush of white, hot molten iron that burst out from the hole, and flowed down across the iron face and the iron bosom— down to the wet rocks, where it fell hissing and sputtering. The huge form stood for a moment swaying and toppling, the iron lips gave forth a terrible, hollow, and ringing cry, and then, turning half around, the giant fell crashing upon the stones, his head in the water, his feet upon the rocky shore. Clouds of hissing steam rose up from the fuming waters where he lay wallowing. Once he strove to rise, lifting his terrible front from the dripping brine. Then he fell again with a splash, rolled over upon his face, and was still, while only a slow, thin vapor rose from his iron length, cooled by the water in which he lay.

David stood towering above his fallen enemy, his bosom heaving and falling as the ocean heaves and falls after the storm has passed by and gone. All had happened so quickly that he could not believe it. Was it true? Yes, it was true! His heart swelled with joy and with triumph as though it would burst. It was true; he had indeed slain the iron monster, that monster that had so long made the earth tremble when he walked upon its quaking bosom. So he stood there, looking down upon the huge fallen form from which the last thin lingering vapor wreaths curled slowly up into the air to melt and to dissolve above.

He heard Phyllis calling him, "David, David!" and then as he turned, lifted up with exaltation, she cried out, "David, the door is open!"

It was true! Now the door was open, and stood ajar, and they might enter when they chose.

David lifted Phyllis up from where she sat, and taking up the Wonder-Box again, thrust the door open and entered.

     .   .   .   .   .

It was the second story of the moon-house.

Phyllis had never seen it before, and she stood gazing about her in the milky brightness, sunk in wonder. "Where are we?" said she.

David looked at her, smiling. "Do you not know?" said he. "This is the moon-house, and we are in the second story. See, there are the windows out of which I used to look and see the wonderful things I sometimes told you about. But, come, Phyllis, let us go down-stairs. I know that the Man-in-the-moon must be waiting for us. Afterward, maybe, we can come back here."

The Man-in-the-moon arose as they came in, and taking off his cap, and holding his long tobacco pipe behind his back, bowed first to David and then to Phyllis. "I am glad to see your Honor's face again," he said to David. "And I am glad to see your Ladyship's pretty face as well, and may you both have a long life and a happy life."

Phyllis blushed and David laughed.

"And what is that you have in your hand?" said the Man-in-the-moon. David held it up. "This," he said, "is the Wonder-Box."

"I was sure you would find it and bring it back again," said the Man-in-the-moon. "I told his Royal Highness, the Master Cobbler, that you would," and the old man smiled until his face was covered all over with a shining cobweb of silvery wrinkles.

"But tell me," said David, "how soon can we get back to the brown earth again? for there is where we wish to go."

"Back to the earth again?" said the Man-in-the-moon,

"How soon?" He looked up at the clock. "Why, you are just in the nick of time. The moon-path will be at its best now in—let me see—in three minutes."

"Then there is no time to lose," said David, "and we must be going."

"I will go down with you," said the Man-in-the-moon.

He led the way down stairs, Phyllis and David following him. Down they went, and down they went, until at last they came to the front door of the moon-house. The Man-in-the-moon opened the door, and there lay the moon-path stretching away across the water, shining as bright as silver, and throwing the light up into their faces.

"Good-bye," said David, and he gave the Man-in-the-moon his hand.

"Good-bye," said the Man-in-the-moon, taking off his hat again as he took David's hand, "I hope you will come to see us again."

"Oh, yes," said David, laughing, "I dare say I'll often be here."

"That's right," said the Man-in-the-moon. "Come again."

David leaped down to the moon-path below. "Come, Phyllis," said he. "Here, you hold the Wonder-Box, and I will help you down." And as he spoke he gave the box to her, and then taking her hand, he lifted her down to the path where he himself stood.

"Good-bye," said the Man-in-the-moon, and hen he closed the door again—Click-clack!

"Come," said David, and then they turned heir faces homeward.

They turned their faces homeward, and—

In an instant Phyllis was gone, and David stood alone, and what was more, she had taken the Wonder-Box with her.

Yes, he was alone. And why was that? Think a moment, and you will see for yourself. This is why she was gone—

Everybody, you see, has a different moon-path from everybody else. David's moon-path led to his home; Phyllis's moon-path led to her home. So, when they began to return back to the brown earth again, one went one way and the other went the other way.

That was why in an instant Phyllis was gone.

David stood looking about him ruefully for a moment, and then he began to laugh.

For he knew that Phyllis was not gone for long. Things do not turn out so in the land of moonshine.

He put up his hand and felt the golden key that hung about his neck. "Oh, well," he said, "it will all turn out right, by and by."

Then he himself started off homeward. At first he walked, then he hurried, then he ran. First it was like walking on a level pasture of silvery light, then it was like hurrying over shifting gravel beneath his feet. Then it was he began to run. The rocky shore came nearer and nearer. Yes; there was Hans Krout sitting on the rocks, looking out toward him. David ran and ran. The golden gravel of brightness began to change to broken bars of light that floated each upon the crest of a wave. Now David was running, leaping from wave to wave. He stepped upon the last wave; the moonlight wriggled and twisted beneath his feet like something alive. Then he jumped stumblingly, regained his footing, and stood upon the rocks of the dear brown earth again.

"How goes it, David?" said Hans Krout.

"It goes well," said David. "How are they at home?"

"They are well," said Hans Krout.

"How is the baby?" said David.

"The baby is thirteen years old," said Hans Krout.

"To be sure she is," said David, "I had forgotten that. Have they missed me from home?" he asked.

"Nobody knows that you have been away," said Hans Krout.

"How long have I been in the moon?" said David.

"You have been there eleven years," said Hans Krout.

"To be sure," said David. He put up his hand to his face. He felt a soft beard on his chin and a moustache on his lip. He looked down at himself. Yes; he had indeed grown into a man. And yet nobody knew that he had been away and had done the greatest work of a hero—that he had slain the Iron Man. Well, that is the way it is in this world often and often.

XVII

David

WHEN David looked about him he saw that it was neither day nor night, but just the twilight betwixt and between—that twilight in which the earth is all bathed in a soft, warm, milky whiteness, that makes everything look bright toward the east, but in which there is no shadow to make what we see look harsh and hard.

David and Hans Krout walked along the rocky path toward the village together. "Did you see the moon-garden?" said Hans Krout.

"Yes; I did," said David.

Hans Krout clucked his tongue behind his teeth. "Ah,"

said he, "I was never able to do that. I was too old."

"Yes," said David, "I suppose you were. I saw you one time and waved my hand to you," he added.

"Yes," said Hans Krout, "I remember. I saw you looking out of the window, and waved my Hans to you, too."

"Yes," said David.

"And where were you for the ten years after that?" said Hans Krout.

"I was behind the Moon-Angel," said David.

"Ah! and did you get there?" said Hans Krout. "Well, I tried it and tried it, but never could get there. I would have given all of the world to have gotten there, but I couldn't."

"That is because you did try," said David. "The way to get there is not to try at all."

"I never thought of that before," said Hans Krout. "Oh, well, I shall get behind the Moon-Angel some time."

"To be sure," said David, "we all of us do." He did not tell Hans Krout whom he had seen and what he had done behind the Moon-Angel.

So they walked together through the twilight, until by and by they had come up over the hill, and there was the village beneath them. Lights were beginning to twinkle, and the geese were squawking, and little children were playing, shouting, and calling with loud voices. There were the boats down upon the shore, and the moon sailing up in the sky like a great round bubble, and laying a wider and wider field of silver across the water. They went past the common, where the children were at play. How strangely familiar it all was—just as it had been eleven years ago. The children pointed at David and Hans Krout, and jeered and laughed at them just as they used to do. "Moon-calf! Moon-calf!" they called; and—

> *"Hans Krout! Hans Krout!*
> *Your wits are out! Your wits are out!"*

David burst out laughing. He did not know any of the children. How should he, seeing that he had been away from home eleven years?

"Have they been calling after me then for all this time?" he asked Hans Krout.

"Yes," said Hans Krout; and he looked up in David's face almost as though he were afraid of him.

There were some young men standing in front of the pot-house, and they grinned at the two as they passed. It seemed to David that he knew them. Yes; one of the men was Tom Stout. The young women they passed laughed at them, too. It seemed strange to David that they should be young women, for when he had left them they were but little girls.

So he walked down the street, and there was his old home. His mother was standing at the door, and her hair had grown as white as silver. He could see his father within the house. He was sitting over the fire, holding his crooked brown hands to the blaze. He had been out fishing and he had not yet got warm.

"Where have you been all this time, David?" said his mother.

"I have been in the moon-house and in the moon-garden, and back of the Moon-Angel," said David.

"Aye, aye; poor boy, poor boy!" said his mother.

His father looked over his shoulder and grunted.

"The same moon-calf as ever," said he.

"Yes," said David, "the same moon-calf as ever," and then again he burst out laughing.

There was not a single one in the whole village, from old Solomon Grundy to David's own father and mother (except Hans Krout), who knew that he had been away from home; still less that he had lived through the most wonderful, strange, incredible, ever-to-be-talked-of adventure that ever a hero faced to come forth from alive.

"And what are you going to do now, David?" said David's mother.

"I am going to wait," said David.

It seemed to her that David was very foolish.

So David sat down to wait.

XVIII

The King's Messenger

S o David the hero waited and waited.

He used to help his father and his mother, and when he was not doing that he was playing with some of the little, little babies of the village. The little babies understood him, though nobody else did. Everybody else laughed at him; even his little sister, whom he used to nurse when she was a baby and who had now grown up into a tall, thin girl of twelve or thirteen—even she laughed at him as did the others in the village, and called him mooncalf. She had forgotten how he had carried her in his arms down to the rocks, and how there both of them had seen the Moon-Angel.

The truth is that the Moon-Angel comes with a sponge at some time to each of us and wipes our memories clean of everything that happens to us from the time we begin to live to the time we are three years old. That is why David's little sister did not remember how they had seen the Moon-Angel together, and that was why she laughed at him now as the others did and called him moon-calf.

But the little babies all understood David, and so he used to play with them.

All that land was in a great hubbub of rejoicing.

The Princess Aurelia, the most beautiful in all the world, had suddenly come back into her senses again, and now she was as wise as anybody else.

That was cause enough of rejoicing, but it was as nothing when it was known that the Wonder-Box and the Know-All Book had been brought back to earth again.

Yes; they had been brought back again, but the box was locked, and there was no key, and no one could open it. All the world knew, however, that the key was to be found, for the Princess told how David had hung it about his neck, and so there was joy and rejoicing.

But who was the hero? who had brought the lost treasure back to the earth again? No one could tell, not even the Princess. "They called him David," said she, "but I do not even know if that was his real name."

"And do you know," said the King, "what has been promised to the hero who shall bring back the Wonder-Box and the Know-All Book?" And then, when the Princess did not reply, he said, "It is that he shall marry you."

The Princess still looked down and raised her pretty eyebrows and blushed, twining her smooth white fingers in and out. "When we were children together in the moon-garden, he told me that it was to be so," said she.

"And are you willing?" said the King. "Are you willing that it should be so?"

"Yes," whispered the Princess Aurelia.

So the King sent out his messengers through all the land to find the hero who had the golden key of the Wonder-Box hung about his neck. For he was to marry the Princess.

Meantime over yonder in the village David waited and waited, for he knew that every beginning must have its ending some time or other.

The King's messengers, each with six knights and a herald, went everywhere—east and west, north and south—to all of the great cities and towns in the kingdom, but nowhere could the hero be found—the man with the golden key hung about his neck.

Then they went to the villages, one after the other; and so, by and by, one of the messengers came to the village where David and his father and mother lived.

It was a grand sight—the King's messenger, the six knights in armor, and the herald with his silver horn with a golden banner hanging from it. The herald sounded his horn as they all marched to the common where the geese fed and the little children played, and there he proclaimed in a loud voice that the King had sent his messenger to find the man who had a golden key hung by a golden chain about his neck."

Everybody crowded about to listen to him, and to gape at him—men, women, and children.

"Have you got it?—Have you got it?—Have you got it?" said the men to one another.

"No; I have not got it,"—"Nor I"—"nor I." Nobody had it.

"Is there any other man living in the village?" asked the King's messenger. Then the people began to laugh. "There is a man named Hans Krout," said one man, "he is a crazy cobbler."

"Bring him hither," said the king's messenger.

Off ran a dozen of them, and presently they returned, bringing Hans Krout with them.

"Have you a golden key hung from your neck by a golden chain?" asked the King's messenger.

"No," said Hans Krout, "such a key as that is all moonshine, and, you see, I was never able to bring any back with me."

"Any what?" said the King's messenger.

"Any moonshine," said Hans Krout.

"Ha-ha-ha!" laughed everybody, and even the King's messenger smiled. They did not know that Hans Krout was the only wise man among them—they all thought he was crazy.

"Is there no other man in the village?" said the King's messenger.

"Why, yes," said one of them that stood near—it was Tom Stout.—"Why, yes, there is one, but he is only a poor, childish creature of a moon-calf. His name is David, and his father and mother are ashamed of him, because he is so simple."

"Nevertheless, bring him hither," said the King's messenger.

The people looked at one another, and laughed.

"Bring him hither," said the King's messenger again, and then a dozen of them ran away to fetch David.

"As soon as they had come into the house, David knew that his waiting had hatched its eggs.

"There's somebody out here who wants to see you," said the people who had come to fetch him.

But David only sat still and smiled. "I cannot go to him," said he.

"But it is the King's messenger," said they.

"I will not go even to the King's messenger," said David. "If he wants me, he must come to me."

They talked and talked to David, but all to no purpose. He would not go, and at last they had to go back to the King's messenger again. "Simpleton has grown proud," said they; "he says that he won't come to you and that you must come to him."

"Very well," said the King's messenger, "then I will go to him."

So off he went across the common, and down the street

to David's house, a great crowd of people following behind
him. There was David sitting, waiting, and when the King's
messenger and the six knights and the herald crowded into
the place, they filled the house. Yes; a noble sight they
were, with silver and gold and bright jewels that gleamed
and glistened and seemed to fill the place with light.

The people who had followed the messenger stood outside and peeped in through the windows, and David's father
and mother stood in the corner and stared, with their eyes
as round as the eyes of fishes. But David sat still, and
looked at the King's messenger and the knights and the
herald, and smiled.

"Have you got a golden key hung about your neck, with
a golden chain?" said the King's messenger.

"Yes; I have," said David.

"Let me see it!" said the King's messenger.

David thrust his hand into his bosom, and there was the
key hung to the golden chain.

"That is it," said the King's messenger. "Blow your horn,
herald!" And the herald blew his horn so loud and shrill
that the rafters cracked and rang.

As for the people peeping in at the windows, they could
not believe their eyes when they saw that David—David
the simpleton—David the moon-calf—really had the
golden key, and was the hero of heroes of whom all the
world was talking.

The King's messenger took off his hat with its fine feathers, and bowed so low that his head almost touched the

floor. And David smiled and put the key back into his bosom again.

"You must come with us now to the King's city," said the King's messenger.

"Yes," said David, "that is what I have been waiting for."

Then they brought up a great white horse with a saddle and bridle sparkling with gold and jewels. The King's messenger himself held the stirrup, while David mounted into the saddle, and the people stood huddled around staring with wonder. David looked around at them and laughed. Poor Tom Stout's eyes were staring like those of a calf, and he looked very droll in his wonder.

Then they rode away and down the street, the horses' hoofs clattering and ringing upon the cobble stones.

"Huzza! huzza!" cried everybody; "Huzza for David the hero!" and they waved their caps above their heads, and some of them threw them in the air. Only the geese upon the common stooped their necks and hissed after the horses' heels. "Huzza! huzza! huzza!" and all the girls waved their handkerchiefs.

So David rode away to the King's palace, and everybody felt proud that such a great hero had been born in that village.

That is the way it happens sometimes.

XIX

Princess Aurelia

*D*AVID, and the King's messenger, and the six knights, and the herald rode away along the highway, over hill and dale, and across the meadows and through the towns and villages, and everybody shouted, "Huzza! huzza!" just as they had done down in the village. "Huzza! huzza! for the hero with the golden key to open the Wonder-Box!" The news of his coming spread like wild-fire, and people came from far and near to catch a glimpse of him as he rode by upon his way.

So at last they came to the King's town.

Thither the news had flown before them, and here, too,

everybody shouted, Huzza! Huzza for the man with the golden key who came to unlock the Wonder-Box!" All the town was packed and crowded as they rode through the streets; the windows were alive with folk looking out, and all was a tumult of waving kerchiefs and flags. As for the cheering, it sounded like the noise of great waters.

And in the midst of it all the hero David rode smiling, and his face shone as white as the moon.

So he rode up the great street of the town, and to the King's palace. And the King himself came out upon the steps to welcome him.

He took David by the hand and led him up the great marble steps, and into the palace, and through the palace to where the Princess Aurelia was waiting. And the lords and nobles, and knights and squires, all dressed in beautiful clothes of gold and silver, with sparkling jewels, made a lane for him up which he was to walk.

The King led him straight to a grand chamber, where was spread a carpet of silver thread, and at the far end sat the Princess Aurelia on a throne. At her right hand was a table, and on it was a box.

It was the Wonder-Box.

She came down the steps to meet him as he came up the steps to meet her. Then she placed her hands on his shoulders and leaned over and kissed him before them all.

All the lords and nobles cheered and shouted, and the King himself took their hands and joined them together.

The Princess led David up to where was the box, and David took the key that hung about his neck by the golden chain, and fitted it in the lock. Everything was hushed to a dead silence. David turned the key and opened the box, and there lay the Know-All Book as white as snow. He opened it, and on the first page were written, in letters of gold, the words—

"When we grow up we shall be married."

Yes; that is what they read when they opened the Wonder-Box; and what followed after, thousands upon thousands of words, told of the same thing—"when we grow up we shall be married; when we are married we shall grow up; when we are married there shall be joy; hence there shall be joy when we are married." Thus it was from the beginning to the end of all there was in the book.

"What!" you say, "was that all?"

Ah, little child, you do not know—you do not know.

The words sound as simple as moonshine, and the foolish man who believes himself wise may laugh to think of a hero going all the way to the other end of nowhere to fetch back nothing more than that written in it. But in all the world, and in all the world to come, there is nothing else that is worth while to write about; for if the yellow heaven had not married the brown earth there would never have been green and blue eyes to the peacock's tail feathers.

Yes; the words are as simple as moonshine, but then you must read them in the Know-All Book to understand what they mean.

Yes; and this that I have told you is not nonsense. The

hero David did indeed bring back the Wonder-Box and the Know-All Book just exactly as I have told you—he did— he did—and those were the words written in it.

Do you not understand? Well, well; some day you may— but first you will have to bathe your eyes with moonshine and then read again.

And were David and the Princess married? Why, of course they were. For the simpleton always marries the Princess in the fairy tales, and that is why they are so true that wise people and little children would rather read them than any- thing else.

And did they ever go back into the moon-garden? Why, of course they did, for those who have read those words in the Know-All Book, and understand what they mean, may go to or come from anywhere, whenever they choose to do so.

Well, you may smile at this story if you choose, and call it all moonshine, but if you do not believe by this time that there is more in moonshine than the glimmer and the white- ness, why, I could not make you believe it if I were to write a hundred and twenty-seven great books instead of this short story.